SUSAN HILL

The Small Hand

and

Dolly

Susan Hill has been a professional writer for over fifty years. Her books have won the Whitbread, the John Llewellyn Prize, and the W. Somerset Maugham Award, and have been shortlisted for the Booker Prize. Her novels include *Strange Meeting*, *I'm the King of the Castle*, and *A Kind Man*, and she has also published autobiography and collections of short stories. Her ghost story, *The Woman in Black*, has been running in London's West End since 1988. Susan is married with two adult daughters and lives in North Norfolk.

www.susan-hill.com

Also by Susan Hill

FICTION

A Kind Man

The Man in the Picture

The Mist in the Mirror

I'm the King of the Castle

In the Springtime of the Year

Strange Meeting

The Woman in Black

SIMON SERRAILLER SERIES

The Various Haunts of Men

The Pure in Heart

The Risk of Darkness

The Vows of Silence

The Shadows in the Street

The Betrayal of Trust

A Question of Identity

NONFICTION

Howards End Is on the Landing:
A Year of Reading from Home

SUSAN HILL

The Small Hand

and

Dolly

TWO NOVELS

VINTAGE BOOKS

A DIVISION OF RANDOM HOUSE, INC.

NEW YORK

FIRST VINTAGE BOOKS EDITION, SEPTEMBER 2013

Copyright © 2010, 2012 by Susan Hill

All rights reserved. Published in the United States by
Vintage Books, a division of Random House, Inc., New York.
The Small Hand was originally published in Great Britain by Profile
Books, London, in 2010, and *Dolly* was originally published in
Great Britain by Profile Books, London, in 2012.

Vintage and colophon are registered trademarks of
Random House, Inc.

Library of Congress Cataloging-in-Publication Data
Hill, Susan.
The Small Hand and Dolly : Two Novels / Susan Hill.
— First Vintage Books Edition.
pages cm
"The Small Hand was originally published in Great Britain
by Profile Books, London, in 2010, and Dolly was
originally published in Great Britain by Profile Books,
London, in 2012"—T. p. verso.
1. Ghost stories. I. Hill, Susan, 1942– Dolly. II. Title.
PR6058.I45S63   2013
823'.914—dc23
2013013552

Vintage ISBN: 978-0-345-80665-9

www.vintagebooks.com

Printed in the United States
10 9 8 7 6 5 4 3 2 1

Contents

The Small Hand   3

The Small Hand   3

Dolly   143

The Small Hand

To Robert, cher ami pour beaucoup d'années,
for so many things
Et aussi pour sa Claudine

One

It was a little before nine o'clock, the sun was setting into a bank of smoky violet cloud and I had lost my way. I reversed the car in a gateway and drove back half a mile to the fingerpost.

I had spent the past twenty-four hours with a client near the coast and was returning to London, but it had clearly been foolish to leave the main route and head across country.

The road had cut through the Downs, pale mounds on either side, and then run into a straight, tree-lined stretch to the crossroads. The fingerpost markings were faded and there were no recent signs. So that when the right turning came I almost shot past it, for there was no sign at all here, just a lane and high banks in which the roots of trees were set deep as ancient teeth. But I thought that this would eventually lead me back to the A road.

The lane narrowed. The sun was behind me, flaring into the rear-view mirror. Then came a sharp bend, the lane turned into a single track and the view ahead was dark beneath overhanging branches.

I slowed. This could not possibly be a way.

Was there a house? Could I find someone to put me on the right road?

I got out. Opposite me was an old sign, almost greened over. THE WHITE HOUSE. Below, someone had tacked up a piece of board. It hung loose but I could just make out the words GARDEN CLOSED in roughly painted lettering.

Well, a house was a house. There would be people. I drove slowly on down the track. The banks were even steeper, the tree trunks vast and elephantine.

Then, at the end of the lane I came out of the trees and into a wide clearing and saw that it was still light after all, the sky a pale enameled silver-blue. There was no through road. Ahead were a wooden gate and a high hedge wound about with briars and brambles.

All I could hear were birds settling down, a thrush singing high up on the branches of a walnut tree and blackbirds pinking as they scurried in the undergrowth. I got out of the car and, as I stood there, the birdsong gradually subsided and then there was an extraordinary hush, a strange quietness into which I felt I had broken as some unwelcome intruder.

I ought to have turned back then. I ought to have retraced my way to the fingerpost and tried again to find the main road. But I did not. I was drawn on, through the gate between the overgrown bushes.

I walked cautiously and for some reason tried not to

make a noise as I pushed aside low branches and strands of bramble. The gate was stuck halfway, dropped on its hinges, so that I could not push it open further and had to ease myself through the gap.

More undergrowth, rhododendron bushes, briar hedge growing through beech. The path was mossed over and grassy but I felt stones here and there beneath my feet.

After a hundred yards or so I came to a dilapidated hut which looked like the remains of an old ticket booth. The shutter was down. The roof had rotted. A rabbit, its scut bright white in the dimness of the bushes, scrabbled out of sight.

I went on. The path broadened out and swung to the right. And there was the house.

It was a solid Edwardian house, long and with a wide verandah. A flight of shallow steps led up to the front door. I was standing on what must once have been a large and well-kept forecourt—there were still some patches of gravel between the weeds and grass. To the right of the house was an archway, half obscured by rose briars, in which was set a wrought-iron gate. I glanced round. The car ticked slightly as the engine cooled.

I should have gone back then. I needed to be in London and I had already lost my way. Clearly the house was deserted and possibly derelict. I would not find anyone here to give me directions.

I went up to the gate in the arch and peered through. I could see nothing but a jungle of more shrubs and bushes, overarching trees, and the line of another path disappearing away into the darkening greenery.

I touched the cold iron latch. It lifted. I pushed. The gate was stuck fast. I put my shoulder to it and it gave a little and rust flaked away at the hinges. I pushed harder and slowly the gate moved, scraping on the ground, opening, opening. I stepped through it and I was inside. Inside a large, overgrown, empty, abandoned garden. To one side, steps led to a terrace and the house.

It was a place which had been left to the air and the weather, the wind, the sun, the rabbits and the birds, left to fall gently, sadly into decay, for stones to crack and paths to be obscured and then to disappear, for windowpanes to let in the rain and birds to nest in the roof. Gradually, it would sink in on itself and then into the earth. How old was this house? A hundred years? In another hundred there would be nothing left of it.

I turned. I could barely see ahead now. Whatever the garden, now "closed," had been, nature had taken it back, covered it with blankets of ivy and trailing strands of creeper, thickened it over with weed, sucked the light and the air out of it so that only the toughest plants could grow and in growing invade and occupy.

I should go back.

But I wanted to know more. I wanted to see more. I wanted for some reason I did not understand to come here in the full light of day, to see everything, uncover what was concealed, reveal what had been hidden. Find out why.

I might not have returned. Most probably, by the time I had made my way back to the main road, as of course I would, and reached London and my comfortable flat, the White House and what I had found there in the dusk of that late evening would have receded to the back of my mind and before long been quite forgotten. Even if I had come this way I might well never have found it again.

And then, as I stood in the gathering stillness and soft spring dusk, something happened. I do not much care whether or not I am believed. That does not matter. I know. That is all. I know, as surely as I know that yesterday morning it rained onto the windowsill of my bedroom after I had left a window slightly open. I know as well as I know that I had a root canal filling in a tooth last Thursday and felt great pain from it when I woke in the night. I know that it happened as well as I know that I had black coffee at breakfast.

I know because if I close my eyes now I feel it happening again, the memory of it is vivid and it is a physical memory. My body feels it, this is not only something in my mind.

I stood in the dim, green-lit clearing and above my head a silver paring of moon cradled the evening star. The birds had fallen silent. There was not the slightest stirring of the air.

And as I stood I felt a small hand creep into my right one, as if a child had come up beside me in the dimness and taken hold of it. It felt cool and its fingers curled themselves trustingly into my palm and rested there, and the small thumb and forefinger tucked my own thumb between them. As a reflex, I bent it over and we stood for a time which was out of time, my own man's hand and the very small hand held as closely together as the hand of a father and his child. But I am not a father and the small child was invisible.

Two

It was after midnight when I got back to London and I was tired, but because what had happened to me was still so clear I did not go to bed until I had got out a couple of maps and tried to trace the road I had taken in error and the lane leading to the deserted house and garden. But nothing was obvious and my maps were not detailed enough. I needed several large-scale Ordnance Survey ones to have any hope of pinpointing an individual house.

I woke just before dawn and as I surfaced from a dreamless sleep I remembered the sensation of the small hand taking hold of my own. But it was a memory. The hand was not there as it had been there, I was now quite sure, in the dusk of that strange garden. There was all the difference in the world, as there was each time I dreamed of it, which I did often during the course of the next few weeks.

I am a dealer in antiquarian books and manuscripts. In the main I look for individual volumes on behalf of clients, at auction and in private sales as well as from other bookmen, though from time to time I also buy speculatively, usually with someone in mind. I do not have shop premises, I work from home. I rarely keep items for very long and I do not have a large store of books for sale at any one time because I deal at the upper end of the market, in volumes worth many thousands of pounds. I do collect books, much more modestly and in a disorganized sort of way, for my own interest and pleasure. My Chelsea flat is filled with them. My resolution every New Year is to halve the number of books I have and every year I fail to keep it. For every dozen I sell or give away, I buy twenty more.

The week after finding the White House saw me in New York and Los Angeles. I then went on trips to Berlin, Toronto and back to New York. I had several important commissions and I was completely absorbed in my undertakings. Yet always, even in the midst of a crowded auction room, or when with a client, on a plane or in a foreign hotel, always and however full my mind was of the job I was engaged upon, I seemed to have some small part of myself in which the memory of the small hand was fresh and immediate. It was almost like a room into which I could go for a moment or two during the day. I was not in the least alarmed or troubled by this. On the contrary, I found it oddly comforting.

I knew that when my present period of travel and activity was over I would return to it and try both to understand what had happened to me and if possible to return to that place to explore and to discover more about it—who had lived there, why it was empty. And whether, if I returned and stood there quietly, the small hand would seek mine again.

I had one disconcerting moment in an airport while buying a newspaper. It was extremely busy and as I queued, first of all someone pushed past me in a rush and almost sent me flying and then, as I was still recovering myself, I felt a child's hand take my own. But when I glanced down I saw that it was the real hand belonging to a real small boy who had clutched me in panic, having also been almost felled by the same precipitate traveler. Within a few seconds he had pulled away from me and was reunited with his mother. The feeling of his hand had been in a way just the same as that of the other child, but it had also been quite different—hot rather than cool, sticky rather than silky. I could not remember when a real child had last taken my hand but it must have been years before. Yet I could distinguish quite clearly between them.

It was mid-June before I had a break from traveling. I had had a profitable few weeks and among other things I had secured two rare Kelmscott Press books for my client in Sussex, together with immaculate signed first editions of all Virginia Woolf's novels, near-mint in their dust wrappers. I was excited to have them and anxious to get them out of my hands and into his. I am well insured, but no amount of money can compensate for the loss or damage of items like these.

So I arranged to drive down with them.

At the back of my mind was the idea that I would leave time to go in search of the White House again.

Three

Was there ever a June as glorious as that one? I had missed too much of the late spring but now we were in the heady days of balmy air and the first flush of roses. They were haymaking as I drove down and when I arrived at my client's house, the garden was lush and tumbling, the beds high and thick with flowers in full bloom, all was bees and honeysuckle and the smell of freshly mown grass.

I had been invited to stay the night and we dined on a terrace from which there was a distant view of the sea. Sir Edgar Merriman was elderly, modest of manner and incalculably rich. His tastes were for books and early scientific instruments and he also had a collection of rare musical boxes which, when wound and set going, charmed the evening air with their sound.

We lingered outside and Sir Edgar's blue-grey coils of cigar smoke wreathed upwards, keeping the insects at bay, the pungent smell mingling with that of the lilies and stocks in the nearby beds. His wife, Alice, sat with us, a small, grey-haired woman with a sweet voice and a shyness which I found most appealing.

At one point the servant came to call Sir Edgar to the telephone and as she and I sat companionably in the soft darkness, the moths pattering around the lamp, I thought to ask her about the White House. Did she know of it? Could she direct me to it again?

She shook her head. "I haven't heard of such a place. How far were you from here?"

"It's hard to tell . . . I was hopelessly lost. I suppose I'd driven for forty-five minutes or so? Perhaps a bit longer. I took a byroad which I thought I knew but did not."

"There are so many unsigned roads in the country. We all know our way about so well, but they are a pitfall for the unwary. I don't think I can help you. Why do you want to go back there, Mr. Snow?"

I had known them both for some four or five years and stayed here overnight once or twice before, but to me they were always Sir Edgar and Lady Merriman and I was always Mr. Snow, never Adam. I rather liked that.

I hesitated. What could I have said? That a deserted and half-derelict house and overgrown garden had some attraction for me, had almost put me under a spell so that I wanted to explore them further? That I was drawn back because . . . how could I have told her about the small hand?

"Oh—you know how some old places have a strange attractiveness. And I might want to retire to the country some day."

She said nothing and, after a moment, her husband returned and the conversation turned back to books and to what he had a mind to buy next. He had wide-ranging tastes and came up with some unusual suggestions. I was always challenged by him, always kept on my toes. He was an exciting client because I could never second-guess him.

"Do you know," he asked now, passing me the decanter, "if another First Folio of Shakespeare is ever likely to come up for sale?"

I almost knocked over my glass.

෴

IT WAS HALF an hour later but the air was still warm as we gathered ourselves to go inside. I was fired with enthusiasm at the same time as I was coolly certain that no First Folio was likely to come my way for Sir Edgar. But even the speculative talk about it had made me think of his wealth in quite new terms.

As I was bidding him goodnight, Lady Merriman said suddenly, "I think I have it, Mr. Snow. I think I have the answer. Do just give me a moment if you would." She went out of the room and I heard her footsteps going up the stairs and away into the depths of the house.

I sat in a low chair beside the open French windows. The lamp was out and a faint whiff of oil came from it. The sky was thick with stars.

And I asked in a low voice, "Who *are* you?" For I had a strange sense of someone being there with me. But of course there was no one. I was alone and it was peaceful and calm.

Eventually, she returned carrying something.

"I am so sorry, Mr. Snow. What we are looking for has always just been moved somewhere else. But this may possibly help you. It came to me as we were sitting there after dinner—the house. The name you gave, the White House, did not register with me because it was always known as Denny's House, to everyone locally—it is about twenty miles from here, but in the country that is local, you know."

She sat down.

"You really shouldn't have gone to any trouble. It was a passing whim. I don't quite know now why it affected me."

"There is an article about it in this magazine. It's rather old. We do keep far too much and I have quite a run of these. The house became known as Denny's House because it belonged to Denny Parsons. Have you heard the name?"

I shook my head.

"How quickly things fall away," she said. "You'll find everything about Denny Parsons and the garden in here." She handed me a *Country Life* of some forty years ago. "Something happened there but it was all hushed up. I don't know any more, I'm afraid. Now, do stay down for as long as you like, Mr. Snow, but if you will excuse me, I am away to my bed."

I went out onto the terrace for a last few moments. Everything had settled for the night, the stars were brilliant, and I thought I could just hear the faint hush of the sea as it folded itself over on the shingle.

ๆ

IN MY ROOM I sat beside my open window with the sweet smell of the garden drifting in and read what Lady Merriman had found for me.

The article was about a remarkable and "important" garden created at the White House by Mrs. Denisa—apparently always known as Denny—Parsons and contained photographs of its creator strolling across lawns and pointing out this or that shrub, looking up into trees. There was also one of those dewy black-and-white portrait photographs popular in such magazines then, of Mrs. Parsons in twinset and pearls, and holding a few delphiniums, rather awkwardly, as if uncertain whether or not to put them down. The soft focus made her look powdery and slightly vacant, but I could see through it to a handsome woman with strong features.

The story seemed straightforward. She had been widowed suddenly when her two children were nine and eleven years old and had decided to move from the Surrey suburbs into the country. When she had found the White House it had been empty and with an overgrown wilderness round it, out of which she had gradually made what was said in the reverential article to be "one of the great gardens of our time."

Then came extensive descriptions of borders and walks and avenues, theater gardens and knot gardens,

of fountains and waterfalls and woodland gardens set
beside cascading streams, with lists of flowers and shrubs,
planting plans and diagrams and three pages of photographs. It certainly looked very splendid, but I am no
gardener and was no judge of the relative "importance"
of Mrs. Parsons's garden.

The place had become well known. People visited
not only from miles away but from other countries. At
the time the article was written it was "open daily from
Wednesday to Sunday for an entrance fee of one shilling
and sixpence."

The prose gushed on and I skimmed some of the more
horticultural paragraphs. But I wanted to know more.
I wanted to know what had happened next. Mrs. Parsons had found a semi-derelict house in the middle of
a jungle. The house in the photographs was handsome
and in good order, with well-raked gravel and mown
grass, fresh paint, open windows, at one of which a pale
upstairs curtain blew out prettily on the breeze.

But the wheel had come full circle. When I had found
the house and garden they were once again abandoned
and decaying. That had happened to many a country
house in the years immediately after the war but it was
uncommon now.

I was not interested in the delights of herbaceous border and pleached lime. The house was handsome in the
photographs, but I had seen it empty and half given over
to wind and rain and the birds and was drawn by it as
I would never have been by somewhere sunny and well
presented.

I set the magazine down on the table. Things change after all, I thought, time does its work, houses are abandoned and sometimes nature reclaims what we have tried to make our own. The White House and garden had had their resurrection and a brief hour in the sun but their bright day was done now.

Yet as I switched out the lamp and lay listening to the soft soughing of the sea, I knew that I would have to go back. I had to find out more. I was not much interested in the garden and house. I wanted to know about the woman who had found it and rescued it yet apparently let it all slip through her fingers again. But most of all, of course, I wanted to go back because of the small hand.

Had Denny Parsons stood there in the gathering dusk, looking at the empty house, surrounded by that green wilderness, and as she made her plans for it felt the invisible small hand creep into her own?

Four

Nothing happened with any connection to the Merrimans or the part of the world in which they lived, and where I had come upon the White House, for several weeks. My trade was going through a dull patch. It happens every so often and ought not to trouble me, but after a short time without any requests from clients or phone calls about possible treasures I become nervous and irritable. If the dead patch continues for longer, I start wondering if I will have to sell some of my own few treasures, convinced that the bottom has dropped out of the business and I will never be active again. Every time it happens I remind myself that things have never failed to turn round, yet I never seem able to learn from experience.

I was not entirely idle of course. I bought and sold one or two complete library sets, including a first edition of Thomas Hardy, and even wondered whether to take up the request from an American collector to find him a full set of the James Bond first editions, mint and in dust wrappers, price immaterial. This is not my field, but I started to ask about in a desultory way, knowing I was probably the hundredth dealer the man had employed to find the Bonds and the one least likely to unearth them.

The summer began to stale. London emptied. I thought half-heartedly of visiting friends in Seattle.

And then two things happened on the same day.

In the post I received an envelope containing a card and a cutting from an old newspaper.

Mr. Snow, I unearthed this clipping about the house, Denny's House, which you came upon by chance when getting lost on your way to us in June. I thought perhaps you might still be interested as it tells a little story. I am sure there is more and if I either remember or read about it again I will let you know. But please throw this away if it is no longer of interest. Just a thought.

Sincerely, Alice Merriman.

I poured a second cup of coffee and picked up the yellowed piece of newspaper.

There was a photograph of a woman whom I recognized as Denisa Parsons, standing beside a large ornamental pool with a youngish man. In the center of the pool was a bronze statue at which they were looking in the slightly artificial manner of all posed photographs.

The statue was of a young boy playing with a dolphin and a golden ball and rose quite beautifully out of the still surface of the water, on which there were one or two water lilies. There might have been fish but none was visible.

The news item was brief. The statue had been commissioned by Denisa Parsons in memory of her grandson, James Harrow, who had been drowned in what was simply described as "a tragic accident." The man with her was the sculptor, whose name was not familiar to me, and the statue was now in place at "Mrs. Parsons's internationally famous White House garden." That was all, apart from a couple of lines about the sculptor's other work.

I looked at the photograph for some time but I could read nothing into the faces, with their rather public smiles, and although the sculpture looked charming to me, I am no art critic.

I put the cutting in a drawer of my desk, sent Lady Merriman a postcard of thanks and then forgot about the whole thing, because by the same post had come a letter from an old friend at the Bodleian Library telling me that he thought he might have news of a Shakespeare First Folio which could conceivably be for sale. If I would like to get in touch . . .

Fifteen minutes later I was in a taxi on my way to Paddington station to catch the next train to Oxford.

Five

"I haven't had an extended lunch break for, what, five years? So I'm taking one today."

It did not surprise me. I have known quite a few librarians across the world, in major libraries and senior posts, and none has ever struck me as likely to take a long lunch, or even in some cases a lunch at all. It is not their way. So I was delighted when Fergus McCreedy, a very senior man at the Bodleian, suggested we walk from there up to lunch at the Old Parsonage. It was a warm, bright summer's day and Oxford was, as ever, crowded. But in August its crowds are different. Parties of tourists trail behind their guide, who holds up a red umbrella or a pom-pom on a stick so as not to lose any of his charges and language-school students on bicycles replace undergraduates on the same. Otherwise, Oxford is Oxford. I always enjoy returning to my old city, so long as I stay no more than a couple of days. Oxford has a way of making one feel old.

Fergus never looks old. Fergus is ageless. He will look the same when he is ninety as he did the day I met him, when we were both eighteen and in our first week at Balliol. He has never left Oxford and he never will. He married a don, Helena, a world expert on some aspect of early Islamic art, they live in a tiny, immaculate house in a lane off the lower Woodstock Road, they take their holidays in countries like Jordan and Turkistan. They have no children, but if they ever did, those children would be, as so many children of Oxford academics have always been, born old.

I had not seen Fergus for a couple of years. We had plenty to catch up on during our walk to lunch and later while we enjoyed a first glass of wine at our quiet table in the Old Parsonage's comfortable dining room. But when our plates of potted crab arrived, I asked Fergus about his letter.

"As you know, I have a very good client who has set me some difficult challenges in the past few years. I have usually found what he wanted—he's a very knowledgeable book collector. It's a pleasure to work with him."

"Not one of the get-me-anything-so-long-as-it-costs-a-lot brigade, then."

"Absolutely not. I have no idea how much he's worth or how he made his money, but it doesn't signify, Fergus, because he loves his books. He's a reader as well as a collector. He appreciates what I find for him. I know I have a living to earn and money is money, but there are some I could barely bring myself to work for."

I meant it. I had had an appalling couple of years being

retained by a Russian oil billionaire who only wanted a book if it was publicized as being both extremely rare and extremely expensive and who did not even want to take delivery of what I bought for him. Everything went straight into a bank vault.

"So your man wants a First Folio."

Our rare fillet of beef, served cold with a new potato and asparagus salad, was set down and we ordered a second glass of Fleurie.

"I told him it was more or less impossible. They're all in libraries."

"We have three," Fergus said. "The Folger has around eighty. Getty bought one a few years ago of course—that was sold by one of our own colleges."

"Oriel. Yes. Great shame."

Fergus shrugged. "They needed the money more than the book. I can understand that. A small private library in London with a mainly theological collection, Dr. Williams's Library, sold its copy a year or so back for two and a half million. But that endows the rest of their collection and saves it for the foreseeable future. It's a question of balancing one thing against another."

"If you had a First Folio would you sell it?"

Fergus smiled. "The one I have in mind as being just possibly for sale does not belong to me. Nor to the Bodleian."

"I thought every one of the 230 or so copies was accounted for?"

"Almost every one. It was thought for some years that apart from all those on record in libraries and colleges and a few in private hands, there was one other First Folio, somewhere in India. But almost by chance, and by following up a few leads, I think I have discovered that that is not the case."

He helped himself to more salad. The room had filled. I looked at the walls, which were lined with an extraordinary assortment of pictures, oils and watercolors, five deep in places—none of them was of major importance but every single one had merit and charm. The collection enhanced the pleasant room considerably.

"The Folio was mentioned to me in passing," Fergus said, "because my German colleague was emailing me about something entirely different, which we have been trying to track down for a long time—a medieval manuscript in fact. In the course of a conversation I had with Dieter, he said almost in passing something like, 'They don't know half of what they do possess, including a Shakespeare First Folio.'"

"They?" I said.

Fergus got up. "Shall we have our coffee on the terrace? I see the sun has come out again."

SITTING AT A TABLE under a large awning, we were somewhat protected from the noise of the passing traffic on the Banbury Road and the coffee was first-rate.

Fergus took three gulps of his double espresso. "Have you ever heard of the monastery of Saint Mathieu des Etoiles?"

"I didn't so much as know there was such a saint."

"Not many do. He's pretty obscure, though there are a couple of churches in France dedicated to him, but so far as I know only one monastery bears his name. It's Cistercian, an enclosed and silent order, and very remote indeed, a bit like La Grande Trappe—high up among mountains and forests, in its own small pocket of time. In winter it can be completely cut off. There is a village some six miles away, but otherwise it's as remote from civilization as you can probably get anywhere in Western Europe. Oh and it also maintains the tradition of wonderful sacred music. A few people do visit—for the music, for a retreat—and the monastery is surprisingly in touch with what you might call our world."

"Most of them are," I said. "I know one in the Appalachian Mountains—remote as they come, but they are on email."

"When you think about it, the silent email suits the rule far better than the telephone. Now, a couple of years ago I had the good fortune to visit Saint Mathieu. They have one of the finest and oldest and best-preserved monastic libraries in the world. One of the ways they earn their living is in book restoration and rebinding for other libraries. We've used their skills occasionally. You're wondering what all this has to do with you? More coffee?"

We ordered. The terrace was emptying out now, as lunchtime drew to a close.

"The monastery, like so many, is in need of money for repairs. When your building dates from the twelfth century things start to wear out. They are not a rich order and the work they do keeps them going, but without anything over and to spare. They urgently need repairs to the chapel frescoes and the roof of the great chapter house, and even though they will provide some of the labor themselves, the monks can't do it all—they don't have the skills and, besides, many of them are in their seventies and older. So, after a great deal of difficulty, they have obtained permission to sell one or two treasures—mainly items which don't have much reason to be there, and which sit rather oddly in a Cistercian monastery. For instance, for some strange reason they have one or two early Islamic items."

"Ah—so Helena comes into the picture."

"She does. So do we. They have a couple of medieval manuscripts, for instance—an Aelfric, a Gilbert of Hoyland. In each case it was thought only one or possibly two copies existed in the world, but Saint Mathieu turns out to have wonderful examples. They only need to sell a few things to pay for all of their repairs and rebuilding and to provide an endowment against future depredations. They're pretty prone to weather damage up there, apart from anything else. They need to protect themselves against future extreme winters."

"It's pretty unusual for items like this to come on the market, Fergus. What else have they got? You make me want to get on the next plane."

He held up his hand. "No. 'The market' is exactly what they do not want to know about any of this. They made contact with us under a seal of total confidentiality. I'm not supposed to be talking to you, so I'd be obliged if you said nothing either."

I was put out. Why tell me at all if my hands were going to be tied as well as my lips sealed?

"Don't sulk." Fergus looked at me shrewdly. "I haven't mentioned this to anyone and I don't intend to—apart from anything else, there would be no point. But the thing is, they have a Shakespeare First Folio—one that was supposed to be somewhere in India. It has never been properly accounted for and my view is that it isn't in India at all but in the Monastery of Saint Mathieu des Etoiles."

"How on earth did they acquire it?"

He shrugged. "Who knows? But in the past when rich young men entered the monastery as postulants their families gave a sort of dowry and it sometimes took the form of art treasures, rare books and so on, as well as of money. That's probably what happened in this case."

"Do they know what they've got?"

"Pretty much. They're neither fools nor innocents. And they are certainly not to be cheated. No, I know you would not, Adam, but your trade is as open to charlatans as any other."

"I like the way you call it 'my' trade."

"Oh, don't look at me," Fergus said, smiling slightly. "I'm just a simple librarian." He stood up. "I've extended my lunch hour far enough. Are you walking back into town?"

He paid the bill and we turned out of the gate and began to walk toward St. Giles.

"The thing is," Fergus said, "some of the items they might conceivably sell will go to America—we simply don't have the money in this country. I am talking to a couple of potential private benefactors but I don't hold out much hope—they get talked to by the world and his wife. Why should they want to give us a single priceless medieval manuscript when they could build the wing of a hospital or endow a chair in medical research? I can't blame them. We've already got First Folios. So have the other libraries. We none of us need another. But you have a client who could presumably afford three or four million to get what he wants?"

"He would never have mentioned it to me if he didn't know how unlikely I was to get one for him, how much it might cost if I ever did and that he could well afford that. He's a gentleman."

"Ah, one of those. Would you like me to get in touch with the monastery and ask one or two discreet questions? I won't mention your name or anything of that kind—and I'll have to work up to it. I think I have the way of them now, but I don't want to pounce or the portcullis will come down."

"And they'll be off to the Huntington Library in a trice."

Fergus's mouth firmed slightly. I laughed.

"You'd all stab one another in the back just as surely as we dealers would," I said. "But thank you, Fergus. And of course, please put in a word. Whatever it takes."

"Yes," he said. "Don't call us and all that."

We parted outside Bodley, Fergus to go into his eyrie

beyond the Duke Humfrey Library, while I went on toward the High. It was a beautiful day now, the air clear and warm, a few clouds like smoke rings high in the sky. There were plenty of trains back to London but I was in no hurry. I thought I would walk down to one of my old favorite haunts, the Botanic Garden, which is surely Oxford's best-kept secret.

Six

I went in through the great gate and began to walk slowly down the wide avenue, looking about me with pleasure, remembering many a happy hour spent here. But it was the Cistercian monastery of Saint Mathieu des Etoiles and its library, as well as the possibility of acquiring a very rare book indeed, which were at the front of my mind. I knew that I could not speak a word of what Fergus had told me, not to Sir Edgar Merriman, nor to a single other soul. I was not such a fool and, besides, I rather wanted to prove to Fergus that antiquarian book dealers are not all charlatans. But I was sure that he had been half-teasing. He knew me well enough.

I wondered how long it would take him to oil his way round to mention of the First Folio in his correspondence with the monastery—presumably by email, as he had hinted. Perhaps not long at all. Perhaps in a day or so I might know whether the business was going to move a step further forward or whether the subject of the Folio would be scotched immediately. There was absolutely nothing I could do but wait.

I had come to the great round lily pond which attends at the junction of several paths. Three or four people were sitting on the benches in the semicircle beside it, enjoying the sunshine. One woman was reading a book, another was knitting. A younger one had a pram in which a baby was sound asleep.

I sat at the end of a bench, still thinking about the Folio, but as I sat, something happened. It is very hard to describe, though it is easy enough to remember. But I had never known any sensation like it and I can feel it still.

I should stress again how at ease I was. I had had a good lunch with an old friend, who had given me a piece of potentially very exciting information. I was in one of my favorite cities, which holds only happy memories for me. The sun was shining. All was right with the world, in fact.

The young woman with the pram had just got up, checked on her baby and strolled off back toward the main gate, leaving the reader, the knitter and me in front of the raised stone pool in which the water lay dark and shining and utterly still.

And at that moment I felt the most dreadful fear. It was not fear of anything, it was simply fear, fear and dread, like a coldness rising up through my body, gripping my chest so that I felt I might not be able to breathe, and stiffening the muscles of my face as if they were frozen. I could feel my heart pounding inside my ribcage, and the waves of its beat roaring through my ears. My mouth was dry and it seemed that my tongue was cleaving to the roof of my mouth. My upper lip and jaw, my neck and shoulder and the whole of my left side felt as if they were being squeezed in a vice and for a split second I believed that I was having a heart attack, except that I felt no pain, and after a second or two the grip eased a little, though it was still hard to breathe. I stood up and began to gasp for air, and I felt my body, which had been as if frozen cold, begin to flush and then to sweat. I was terrified. But of what, of what? Nothing had happened. I had seen nothing, heard nothing. The day was as sunlit as before, the little white clouds sailed carelessly in the sky and one or two of them were reflected in the surface of the still pool.

And then I felt something else. I had an overwhelming urge to go close to the pool, to stand beside the stone rim and peer into the water. I realized what was happening to me. Some years ago, Hugo, my brother and older than me by six years, went through a mental breakdown from which it took him a couple of years to recover. He had told me that in the weeks before he was forced to seek medical help and, indeed, to be admitted to hospital, almost the worst among many dreadful experiences was of feeling an overwhelming urge to throw himself off the edge of the underground station platform into the path of a train. When he was so afraid of succumbing to its insistence he walked everywhere, he felt he must step off the pavement into the path of the traffic.

He stayed at home, only to be overwhelmed again, this time by the urge to throw himself out of the window onto the pavement below.

And now it was happening to me. I felt as if I was being forced forward by a power outside myself. And what this power wanted me to do was throw myself face down into the great deep pool. As I felt the push from behind so I felt a powerful magnetic force pulling me forward. The draw seemed to be coming from the pool itself and between the two forces I was totally powerless. I think that I was split seconds from flinging myself forward into and under the dark water when the woman who had been knitting suddenly started up, flapping at a wasp. Her movement broke the spell and I felt everything relax, the power shrink and shrivel back, leaving me standing in the middle of the path, a yard or so from the pool. A couple were walking toward me, hand in hand. A light aircraft puttered slowly overhead. A breeze blew.

Slowly, slowly, the fear drained out of me, though I felt shaken and light-headed, so that I backed away and sat down again on the bench to recover myself.

I stayed for perhaps twenty minutes. It took as long as this for me to feel calm again. As I sat there in the sunshine, I thought of Hugo. I had never fully understood until now how terrifying his ordeal had been, and how the terrors must have taken him over, mentally and physically. No wonder he had said to me when I first visited him in the hospital that he felt safe for the first time in several years.

Was it hereditary, then? Was I about to experience these terrifying urges to throw myself out of windows or into the path of oncoming trains? I knew that Hugo had gone through a very turbulent time in his youth and I had put his condition down to a deep-seated reaction to that. So far as I knew, neither of our parents had ever suffered in the same way.

At last, I managed to get up and walk toward the gates. I felt better with every step. The fear was receding rapidly. I only shivered slightly as I looked back at the pool. Nothing more.

I was glad to be in the bustle of the High and I had no urge whatsoever to throw myself under a bus. I walked briskly to the railway station and caught the next train back to London.

THAT NIGHT I DREAMED that I was swimming underwater, among shimmering fish with gold and silver iridescent bodies which glided past me and around me in the cool, dark water. For a while, it was beautiful. I felt soothed and lulled. I thought I heard faint music. But then I was no longer swimming, I was drowning. I had seemed to be like a fish myself, able to breathe beneath the surface, but suddenly the air was being pressed out of my lungs by a fast inflow of water and I was gasping, with a painful sensation in my chest and a dreadful pulsing behind my eyes.

I came to in the darkness of my bedroom, reached

out to switch on the lamp and then sat, taking in great draughts of air. I got up and went to the window, opened it and breathed in the cool London night, and the smell of the trees and grass in the communal gardens of the square. I supposed the panic which had overcome me beside the pool in the Botanic Garden had inevitably left its traces in my subconscious, so that it was not surprising these had metamorphosed into night horrors.

But it faded quickly, just as the terror of the afternoon had faded. I am generally of an equable temperament and I was restored to my normal spirits quite easily. I was only puzzled that I should have had such an attack of panic out of the blue, followed by a nightmare from which I had surfaced thrashing in fear. I had had a pleasant day and I was excited about Fergus's possible coup. The tenor of my life was as even and pleasant as always.

The only untoward thing that had happened to me recently was the incident in the garden of the White House. Unlike the terror and the nightmare, the memory of that had not faded—indeed, if anything it was clearer. I closed my eyes and felt again the small hand in mine. I could almost fold my fingers over it, so real, so vivid was the sensation.

Without quite knowing that I was going to do so then, I did fold my fingers over as if to enclose it. But there was nothing.

Not this time. Not tonight.

Seven

My business was going through the usual summer lull and I did not have enough to occupy me. The nightmare did not return, but although I had no more attacks of fear, I could not get that experience out of my mind and, in the end, I decided that I would talk to my brother. I rang to ask if I could go to see them for a night and got his Danish wife, Benedicte, who was always welcoming. I think that so far as she was concerned I could have turned up on their doorstep at any time of the day or night and I would have been welcome. With Hugo, though, it was different.

He was now a teacher in a boys' public school situated in a pleasant market town in Suffolk. They had a Georgian house with a garden running down to the river and the slight air of being out of time that always seems to be part of such places.

They had one daughter, Katerina, who had just left to

stay with her cousins in Denmark for the holiday. Hugo and Benedicte were going to the States, where he was to teach a summer school.

I have always felt a great calm and contentment as I step through their front door. The house is light and elegant and always immaculate. But if it belongs to the eighteenth century from the outside, within it is modern Scandinavian, with a lot of pale wood flooring, cream rugs, cream leather chairs, steel and chrome. It would be soulless were it not for two things. The warmth that emanates from Benedicte herself, and the richly colored wall hangings which she weaves and sells. They make the house sing with scarlet and regal purple, deep blue and emerald.

It is a strange environment for my brother. Hugo has perhaps never quite picked up the last threads of equilibrium, which is why the house and his wife are so good for him. He has an edginess, a tendency to disappear inside himself and look into some painful distance, detached from what is going on around him. But he loves his job and his family and I do not think he is greatly troubled—for all that he has reminders of his sufferings from time to time.

❧

I ARRIVED IN the late afternoon and caught up on news. Benedicte was going out to her orchestra practice— she plays the oboe—but left us with a delicious dinner which needed only a few final touches put to it. The kitchen opened on to the garden, with a distant glimpse of the river, and it was warm enough for us to have the doors open on to a still evening. The flames of the candles in their slender silver holders scarcely flickered.

"I need your advice," I said to Hugo, as we began to eat our smoked fish. "Advice, help—I'm really not sure which."

He looked across at me. We are not alike. Hugo takes after our mother, in being tall and dark with a long oval face. I am stockier and fairer, though we are of a height. But our eyes are the same, a deep smoky blue. Looking into Hugo's eyes was oddly like looking into my own in a mirror. How much else of his depths might I see in myself, I wondered.

"Do you ever . . ." I looked at the fish on my fork. I did not know how to ask, what words to use that would not upset him. "I wonder if you sometimes . . ."

He was looking straight at me, the blue eyes direct and as unwavering as the candle flames. But he was silent. He gave me no help.

"The thing is . . . something quite nasty happened to me. Nothing like it has ever happened before. Not to me. Nothing . . ." I heard my voice trailing off into silence.

After a moment Hugo said, "Go on."

As if a torrent had been unleashed, I began to tell him about the afternoon in the Botanic Garden and my terrible fear and then the overwhelming urge to fall face down into the water. I told him everything about the day, I elaborated on my feelings leading up to the fear,

I went into some detail about how things were in my present life. The only thing I did not mention, because there were somehow not the words to describe it, was the small hand.

Hugo listened without interrupting. We helped ourselves to chicken pie. A salad.

I fell silent. Hugo took a piece of bread. Outside it had grown quite dark. It was warm. It was very still. I remembered the night I had sat out on the terrace at the Merrimans' house in the gathering dusk, so soon after these strange events had begun.

"And you think you are going mad," Hugo said evenly. "Like me."

"No. Of course I don't."

"Oh, come on, Adam . . . If you're here to get my advice or whatever it is you want, tell me the truth."

"I'm sorry. But the truth is—well, I don't know what it is, but you didn't go mad."

"Yes, I did. Whatever 'mad' is, I went it to some degree. I was in a madhouse, for God's sake."

I had never heard him speak so harshly.

"Sorry," I said.

"It's fine. I hardly think about it now. It's long gone. Yet there is sometimes the shadow of a shadow, and when that happens I wonder if it could come back. And I don't know, because I don't know what caused it in the first place. My psyche was turned inside out and shaken, but they never got to the bottom of why."

He looked at me speculatively. "So now you." Then, seeing my expression, he added quickly, "Sorry, Adam.

Of course not you. What you had was just a panic attack."

"But I've never had such a thing in my life."

He shrugged. A great, soft, pale moth had come in through the open window and was pattering round the lamp. I have never cared for moths.

"Let's go out for some air," I said.

It was easier, strolling beside my brother down the garden. I could talk without having to see his face.

"Why would I have what you call a panic attack, out of the blue? What would cause it?"

"I've no idea. Perhaps you're not well?"

"I'm perfectly well."

"Shouldn't you see your GP all the same, get a check?"

"I suppose I could. When you . . ."

"No," he said, "I wasn't ill either."

We stood at the bottom of the path. A few paces away was the dark river.

"I was within a hair's breadth of throwing myself into that pool. It was terrifying. It was as if I had to do it, something was making me."

"Yes."

"I'm afraid it will happen again."

He put a hand briefly on my shoulder. "Go and see someone. But it probably won't, you know."

"Did you ever ask if anyone else in the family had had these—attacks, these fears?"

"Yes. So far as anyone knew, they didn't."

"Oh."

"I think that part really is coincidence."

"I might not be able to resist another time."

"I'm pretty sure you will."

"Might you have jumped in front of one of those trains?"

"I think . . ." he said carefully, "that there was usually something inside me that held me back—something stronger than it, whatever 'it' was. But once . . . once perhaps." He shook himself. "I'd rather not."

"The shadow of a shadow."

"Yes."

We heard the sound of Benedicte's car pulling up and then the bang of the front door. Hugo turned to go back inside. I did not. I walked on, beyond the end of the garden and across the narrow path until I was standing on the riverbank. I could smell the water, and although there was only a half-moon, the surface of it shone faintly. I felt calm now, calm and relieved. Hugo seemed to have come through his own ordeal unscathed. He did not want to dwell on it and I couldn't blame him. I think I knew that whatever had happened to me was of a different order and with a quite different origin. I also knew that if ever it happened to me again, my brother would not want to help me. Nothing had been said and in all other respects I knew I would always be able to rely on him, as I hoped he would upon me. But in this, I was alone.

Or perhaps not alone.

I heard the water lap the side of the bank softly. I felt no fear of it. Why should I?

I waited for some time there in the darkness. I heard

their voices from the house. A door closed. A light went on upstairs.

I waited until I felt the night chill off the water and then I turned away with what I realized was a sort of sadness, a disappointment that the small hand had not crept into mine. I was coming to expect it.

I still had the sense then that the hand belonged to someone whose intentions were wholly benign and who was well disposed toward me, who was trusting.

I WAS TO look back on that night with longing—longing for the sense of peace I knew then, even if I also felt an odd sudden loneliness; even if I had, God help me, for some strange reason actually hoped for the presence of the small hand holding mine.

Eight

The following night I had another vivid dream. I was standing as I had stood that evening beside the broken-down gate that led into the garden of the White House, only this time it was not evening but night, a cold, clear night with a sky sown with glittering stars. I was alone and I was waiting. I knew that I was waiting but for whom I waited the dream did not tell me. I felt excited, keyed up, as if some longed-for excitement was about to happen or I was to see something very beautiful, experience some great pleasure.

After a time, I knew that someone was coming toward me from the depths of the garden beyond the gate, though I neither heard nor saw anything. But there was a small light bobbing in the darkness among the trees and bushes some way ahead and I knew that it was getting nearer. Perhaps someone was carrying a lantern.

I waited. In a moment, whoever it was would appear

or call out to me. I was eager to see them. They were bringing me something—not an object but some news or information. They were going to tell me something and when they had told me, everything would fall into place. I would know a great secret.

The light disappeared now and then, as the undergrowth obscured it, but then I saw it again a little nearer to me. I moved a step or two forward, my hand on the broken gate. I can feel it now, the cool roughened wood under my palm. I can see the lamp growing a little brighter.

I felt a great wave of happiness and, at the same time, a desire to run toward the light, to push my way roughly through the branches that hung low over the path. I had to do so. I was needed. It was urgent that I should go into the garden, that I should meet the lantern-bearer, that I should not waste another moment, as I somehow felt that I had wasted so many—not moments, but months and years.

I pushed on the gate to try and free it from where it was embedded in the earth and grass, which had grown up in great coarse clumps around it.

I was not pushing hard enough. The gate did not budge. I put my shoulder to it. I had to open it and go into the garden, go quickly, because now the light was very near but going crazily from side to side, as if someone was swinging it hard.

I put my whole strength to the gate and pushed. It gave suddenly so that I was pitched forward and felt myself falling.

And as I fell, I woke.

꙳

I THOUGHT A GREAT deal about the dream in the course of the next couple of days and instead of fading from my mind the memory of it became stronger. Perhaps if I could find out more about the White House and its garden, and if I went there again, I would be able to loosen the strange hold it seemed to have on me.

I would pay a visit to the London Library, and if that yielded nothing the library of the RHS, and try to find anything that had been written about it. I had no interest in gardens but something had led me to the ruins of that one and something had happened to me during those few minutes I had spent there which was haunting me now.

Before I had a chance to get to any library, however, a phone call from Fergus McCreedy put the whole matter from my mind.

"I have news for you," he said.

꙳

THE MONASTERY OF Saint Mathieu des Etoiles clearly trusted Fergus. The Librarian had sent him a confidential list of the treasures they felt able to sell to raise the money they needed. They included, he said, two icons, the Islamic objects in which Helena was so interested, and three medieval manuscripts. And a Shakespeare First Folio. The Librarian had asked Fergus if he would act as go-between in the disposal of the items—they wanted someone who had an entrée to libraries, museums and collectors round the world, who could be trusted not to send out a press release, and above all a man they regarded as fair and honorable. Fergus was to visit the monastery later in the summer, to look at everything, but he had proposed that I be allowed to go there at once, specifically to look at the First Folio. He had told the Librarian about me. My credentials seemed to satisfy and Fergus suggested I make arrangements with the monastery to visit as soon as I could. If I agreed, he proposed to forward all the contact details.

"It is a silent order," he said, "but the Librarian and the Guest Master are allowed to talk in the course of their duties, and both speak English. I suggest you get on with it."

I asked if that meant he thought they might change their minds.

"Not at all. It has been deliberated over for a long time. They are quite sure and the Head of the Order has approved it all. But you don't want anyone else to get wind of this and neither do I. In my experience things have a way of getting out, even from enclosed orders of silent monks."

Nine

I started on my journey in a mood of cheerfulness and optimism. The shadows had blown away. The sun had come out. I needed a break, which was why I flew to Lyons and then hired a car, for I planned to take my time, meandering on country roads, staying for two or three nights in different small towns and villages, enjoying France. I knew parts of the country well but not the region in which the monastery of Saint Mathieu des Etoiles was situated, high up in the mountains of the Vercors. I was ready to explore, pleased to be going on what I thought of as a pleasant jaunt and with the prospect of discovering a rare and wonderful book to delight a client at the end of it.

I hardly recognize the person I was at the beginning of that journey. It is true I had had a strange encounter and been touched by some shadow, but I had pushed them to the back of my mind; they had not changed me as I was later to be changed. I was able to forget. Now, I cannot.

I see those few days in a sunlit France as being days of light before the darkness, days of tranquillity and calm before the gathering storm. Days of innocence, perhaps.

It was high summer and hot, but the air was clear and, as always in such weather, the countryside looked its best, welcoming and uplifting to the spirits. There were pastures and gentle hills, charming villages. One night I had a room above an old stable in which chickens scratched contentedly and swallows were nesting. In the morning, I woke to lie looking across a distant line of violet-colored hills. I was heading toward them that day. They seemed like pictures in a child's book.

I ate modestly at breakfast and lunch, but always stopped in time to dine well, so that I slept seven or eight hours, deep draughts of dreamless sleep.

By the time I was on the road for the third morning, the weather had begun to change. The sun shone for the first half-hour or so, but as I climbed higher I drove into patches of thin, swirling mist. It was very humid and I could see dark and heavy clouds gathering around the mountains ahead. Earlier, I had driven through many a small and pleasant village and seen people about, in the streets, working in the fields, cycling, walking, but now I was leaving human habitations behind. Several times I passed small roadside shrines, commemorating the wartime dead of the Resistance, which had been so strong in these parts. Once, an old woman was putting fresh flowers into the metal vase clipped to one of them. I waved to her. She stared but did not respond.

The roads became steeper and the bends sharper. The

clouds were darkening. I passed through several short tunnels cut from the rock. On either side of me, the cliffs began to tower up, granite grey with only the odd fern or tree root clinging to its foothold. The car stuttered once or twice and I needed all my concentration to steer round some of the bends that coiled like snakes, up and up.

But then I came out onto a narrow plateau. The sky was darkening but to my right a thin blade of sunlight shot for a second down through the valley below. Somewhere, it caught water and the water gleamed. But then great drops of rain began to fall and a zigzag of blue-white lightning ran down the side of the rock. I was unsure whether to wait or to press on, but the road was narrow and I could not safely pull in to the side. I had not seen another vehicle for several miles but if one came up behind me, especially in the darkness and now blinding rain of the storm, it would certainly crash into me. I drove on extremely slowly. The rain was slanting sideways so that my windscreen was strangely clear. More lightning and still more streaking down the sulphurous-looking sky and arcing onto the road. I could not tell whether what was roaring on the car roof was rain or thunder.

The road was still narrow but now, instead of climbing I began to descend, skirting the highest part of the mountain and heading toward several lower slopes, their sides thickly overgrown with pine trees.

The rain was at my back and seemed to be coming out of a whirlwind which drove the car forward.

I am a perfectly calm driver and I had driven in atrocious conditions before then, but now I was afraid. The narrowness of the road, the way the storm and the high rocks seemed to be pressing down upon me at once, together with the tremendous noise, combined to unnerve me almost completely. I was conscious that I was alone, perhaps for many miles, and that although I had a map I had been warned that the monastery was difficult to find. I thought I had perhaps another twenty miles to go before I turned off on the track that led to Saint Mathieu, but I might well miss it in such weather.

Two things happened then.

Once again, in the midst of that black, swirling storm, a blade of sunlight somehow pierced its way through the dense cloud. This time I almost mistook it for another flash of lightning as it slanted down the rock face to my left and across the road ahead, which had the astonishing effect of turning the teeming rain into a thousand fragments of rainbow colors. It lasted for only a second or two before the clouds overwhelmed it again, but it was during those seconds that I saw the child. I was driving slowly. The road was awash and I could not see far ahead. But the child was there. I had no doubt of that then. I have no doubt of it now.

One moment there was only rain, bouncing up off the road surface, pouring down the steep sides of the cliff beside the car. Then, in the sudden shaft of sunlight, there was the child. He seemed to run down a narrow track at the side of the road between some overhanging trees and dash across in front of me. I braked, swerved, shouted, all at the same moment. The car slid sideways and came to a halt at the roadside, nose toward the rocks. I leaped out, disregarding the rain and the storm still raging overhead. I did not see how I could have avoided hitting the child, it had been so near to me, though I had felt no impact. I had not seen him—I was sure that it was a boy—fall but surely he must have done so. Perhaps he was beneath the car, lying injured.

Such violent storms blow themselves out very quickly in the mountains and I could see the veils of rain sweeping away from the valley ahead and it grew lighter as the clouds lifted. The thunder cracked above me but the lightning was less vivid now.

One glance under the car told me that the body of the child was not lying in the road beneath it. There was no mark on the front.

I looked round. I saw the track between the pine trees down which he must have come running. So he had raced in front of the car, missing it by inches, and presumably down some path on the opposite side.

I crossed the road. The thunder grumbled away to my right. Steam began to rise from the surface of the road and wisps of cloud drifted across in front of me like ectoplasm.

"Where are you?" I shouted. "Are you all right? Call to me." I shouted again, this time in French.

I was standing on a patch of rough grass a few yards away from the car on the opposite side. Behind rose the jagged bare surface of rock. I turned and looked down. I was standing on the edge of a precipice. Below me was a sheer drop to a gorge below. I glimpsed dark water and the cliffs on the far side before I stepped back in terror. As I stepped, I missed my footing and almost fell but managed to right myself and leap across the road toward the safety of the car. As I did so, I felt quite unmistakably the small hand in mine. But this time it was not nestling gently within my own, it held me in a vicious grip and as it held so I felt myself pulled toward the edge of the precipice. It is difficult to describe how determined and relentless the urging of the hand was, how powerful the force of something I could not see. The strength was that of a grown man although the hand was still that of a child and at the same time as I was pulled I felt myself in some strange way being urged, coaxed, guided to the edge. If I could not be taken by force, then it was as though I were to be seduced to the precipice and into the gorge below.

The storm had rolled away now and the air was thick with moisture which hung heavily about me so that I could hardly breathe. I could hear the sound of rushing water and the rumble of stones down the hillside not far away. The torrent must have dislodged something higher up. I was desperate to get back into the safety of the car but I could not shake off the hand. What had happened to the child I could not imagine, but I had seen no pathway and if he had leaped, then he must have fallen. But where had a child come from in this desolate and empty landscape and in the middle of such a storm, and how had he managed to avoid being hit by my car and disappear over the edge of a precipice?

I wrenched my hand as hard as I could out of the grip of the invisible one. I felt as if I were resisting a great magnetic force, but somehow I stumbled backward across the road and then managed to free my hand and get into the car. I slammed the door behind me in panic and, as I slammed it, I heard a howl. It was a howl of pain and rage and anguish combined, and without question the howl of a furious child.

Ten

My map was inadequate and there were no signs. I was shaking as I drove and had to keep telling myself that whatever might have happened, I had not killed or injured any child nor allowed myself to be lured over the precipice to my death. The storm was over but the day did not recover its spirits. The sky remained leaden, the air vaporous. From time to time, the curtain of cloud came down, making visibility difficult. Twice I took a wrong turning and was forced to find a way of retracing my route. I saw no one except a solitary man leading a herd of goats across a remote field.

After an hour and a half, I rounded a sharp bend, drove through one of the many tunnels cut into the rock and then saw a turning to the left, beside another of the little shrines. I stopped and consulted my map. If this was not the way to the monastery, I would press on another six miles to the next village and find someone to ask.

The narrow lane ran between high banks and through

gloomy pine trees whose slender trunks rose up ahead and on either side of my car, one after another after another. After being level for some way, it began to twist and climb, and then to descend before climbing again. Then, quite suddenly, I came out into a broad clearing. Ahead of me was a small wooden sign surmounted by a cross: MONASTERE DE SAINT MATHIEU DES ETOILES. VOITURES.

I switched off the engine and got out of the car. The smell of moist earth and pine needles was intense. Now and again a few raindrops rolled down the tree trunks and pattered onto the ground. Thunder grumbled but it was some distance away. Otherwise, everything was silent. And I was transported back on the instant to the evening I had stood outside the gate of the White House and its secret, overgrown garden. I had the same sense of strangeness and isolation from the rest of the world.

I was expected at the monastery. I had had email correspondence with the Librarian and been assured that a guest room would be made available for me at any time. They had very few visitors and those mainly monks from other houses. The Librarian, Dom Martin, had attached a helpful set of notes about the monastery and its way of life. I would be able to speak only to him and (although it was possible I would also be received by the Abbot), to the Guest Master, might attend the services in the chapel and would be given access to the library. But this was an enclosed and silent order and, though I was welcome, I would be kept within bounds.

"C'est probable," the Librarian had written, "que vous serez ici tout seul."

Now I took my bag from the car and set off down the narrow path through the dense and silent pines. I was still suffering from the effects of what had happened, but I was glad to have arrived at a place of safety where there would be other human beings, albeit silent and for the most part unapproachable. A monastery was holy ground. Surely nothing bad could happen to me here.

The track wound on for perhaps half a mile and for most of the way it was monotonous, rows of pines giving way to yet more. At first it was level, then I began to climb, and then to climb quite steeply. The only sound was the soft crunch of my own footsteps on the pine-needle floor. There were no birds, though in the distance I could hear falling water, as if a stream were tumbling down over rocks. The air was humid but as I climbed higher it cleared and even felt chill, which was a welcome relief. I imagined this place in deep winter, when the snow would make the track impassable and muffle what few sounds there were.

I stopped a couple of times to catch my breath. I walk about London and other cities a great deal, but that is easy walking and does not prepare one for such a steep climb. I wiped my face on my jacket sleeve and carried on.

And then, quite suddenly, I was out from between the trees and looking down the slope of a stony outcrop on to the monastery of Saint Mathieu des Etoiles.

The roofs were of dark grey shingle and the whole formed an enclosed rectangle with two single buildings on the short sides, one of which had a high bell tower. The long sides were each divided into two dozen identical units. There was a second, smaller rectangle of buildings to the north. The whole was set on the level and surrounded by several small fenced pastures, but beyond these the ground was sheer, climbing to several high peaks. The slopes were pine-forested. The sun came out for a moment, bathing the whole in a pleasant and tranquil light. The sky was blue above the peaks, though there were also skeins of cloud weaving between them. I heard the tinkle of a cowbell, of the sort that rings gently all summer through the Swiss Alps. A bee droned on a ragged purple plant at my feet. The rest was the most deep and intense silence.

I stood, getting my breath and bearings, the canvas bag slung across my shoulders, and for the first time that day I felt a slight lifting of the fear that had oppressed me. And I also recalled that somewhere in that compact group of ancient buildings below were the most extraordinary treasures, books, icons, pictures—who knew what else?

I shifted the bag onto my left shoulder and began to make my way carefully down the steep and rocky path toward the monastery.

❧

I DO NOT know what I expected. The place was silent save for a single bell tolling as I approached the gate. It stopped and all I could hear were those faint natural sounds, the rain dripping off roofs and trees, the stream.

But when the door in the great wooden gate was opened to me and I gave my name, I was greeted by a smiling, burly monk in a black hooded habit and a large cotton apron. He greeted me in English.

"You are welcome, Monsieur Snow. I am Frère Jean-Marc, the Guest Master. Please . . ."—and he took my bag from me, lifting it as if it contained air and feathers.

He asked me where I had left my car and nodded approval as he led me across an inner courtyard toward a three-story building.

Every sound had its own resonance in such a silent atmosphere. Our footsteps, separate and in rhythm, the monk's slight cough, another bell.

"You have come a long way to visit us."

"Yes. I also came through a terrible storm just now."

"Ah, mais oui, the rain, the rain. But our storms go as quickly as they come. It's the mountains."

"The road is treacherous. I'm not used to such bends."

He laughed. "Well, you are here. You are welcome."

We had climbed three flights of stone stairs and walked along a short corridor to the door which he now opened, standing aside to let me pass.

"Welcome," he said again.

I felt real warmth in his greeting. Hospitality to strangers was an important part of the monastic rule, for all that these monks did not receive many.

I walked into the small, square room. The window opposite looked directly onto the pine-covered slopes and the jagged mountain peak. The sun was out, slanting toward us and lighting the deep, dark green of the trees, catching the whitewashed stone walls of the surrounding monastery buildings.

"Ah," the Guest Master said, beaming, "beautiful. But you should see it in the snow. That is a sight."

"I imagine you have few guests in winter."

"None, Monsieur. For some months we are impassable. Now, here . . . your bed. Table. Your chair. On here you see a letter from the Abbot to you, a letter also from Dom Martin, the Librarian. This list is our timetable. Here is a small map. But I will fetch you at the times you will meet. You are welcome to walk outside anywhere save the private cloister. You are welcome, most welcome, to attend any service in the chapel and I will take you in half an hour, to show you where this is, where you may sit, the dining room. But for now I will bring you refreshment in this room, so that you may get used to the place. You will meet the brothers also about the monastery, the brothers at work. Of course, please greet them. They are glad to welcome a guest. Now, I will leave you to become at home, and I will return with some food and drink."

The room was peaceful. The sun moved round to shine on the white wall and the white cover of the iron-framed single bed. The window was open slightly. I could hear the distant sound of the cowbells.

For a moment, I thought that I would weep.

Instead, the walls seemed to shimmer and fold in upon themselves like a pack of cards and I fainted at Frère Jean-Marc's feet.

Eleven

I woke to find myself lying on the bed with the kindly and concerned face of the Guest Master looking down on me. There was another monk on my left side, holding my wrist to take the pulse, an older man with wrinkled, parchment-like skin and soft blue eyes.

"Now, Monsieur Snow, lie still, relax, You gave us a great shock. This is Dom Benoît, our Infirmarian. Il est médecin. His English is a little less than mine."

I struggled to sit up but the old man restrained me gently. "Un moment," he said. "You do not race away . . ."

I lay back. Through the window I could see the mountain peak and a translucent blue sky. I felt strangely calm and at peace.

❦

IN THE END, Dom Benoît seemed to decide that I was none the worse for my fainting attack and allowed me to sit up. There was a tray of food on the table by the window, with a carafe of water, and I went to it after both men had left, feeling suddenly hungry. The Guest Master had said that I should rest for the afternoon, sleep if possible, and that he would come back later to check up on me and, if the Infirmarian agreed, take me to my appointment with the Librarian.

I ate a bowl of thick vegetable soup that tasted strongly of celery, some creamy Brie-like cheese and fresh bread, a small salad and a bowl of cherries and grapes. The water must have come from a spring in the mountains—it had the unmistakable coolness and fresh taste that only such water has.

I felt perfectly well now, but slightly light-headed. I supposed that I had fainted in the aftermath of the morning's awful drive, though I do not remember ever passing out in my life before. I noticed that there was a faint redness on my upper arm where Dom Benoît had probably taken my blood pressure. I was being looked after with care.

As I ate I looked at the letters that had been left for me. The first, from the Librarian, suggested a meeting that evening, when he would be glad to show me both the First Folio and any other books I might like to see. I would also be welcome to visit the book bindery. The letter from the Abbot was brief, formal and courteous, simply bidding me welcome and hoping that he would be able to see me at some point during my stay.

The timetable, which had been typed out to give me an idea of how the monastic day and night were organized, was a formidable one. There was a daily mass, all the usual offices, the angelus and much time for private prayer and meditation. The monks ate together only once a day, in the evening, otherwise meals were taken in the solitude of their cells, or at their work.

There was a map of both the inside and the outside of the monastery, with a dotted red line, or cross, indicating areas to which I did not have access. But I was free to walk almost anywhere outside. I could go into the chapel, the refectory, the library and the communal areas of the cloisters. It seemed that I was also free to visit the kitchens and the carpentry shops and the cellars, the dairy and the cowsheds if I wished.

When I began to eat I had thought I would take a walk in the grounds near to the buildings as soon as I had finished the last mouthful. But I had barely begun to eat the fruit when a tiredness came over me that made my head swim and my limbs feel as heavy as if they had been filled with sawdust.

I opened the window more, so that the sweet air blew in from the mountain, with a breath of pine. Then I lay down and, to the gentle sound of the cowbells, I fell into the deepest sleep I have ever known.

I WOKE INTO a soft mauve twilight. The stars had come out behind the mountain and there was a full moon. I lay still, enjoying the extraordinary silence. The morning's drive through the storm and the horror of almost running over the child seemed to belong to another time. I felt as if I had been in this small, white-washed, peaceful room for weeks. After a few moments, I heard the bell sound somewhere in the monastery, calling the monks to more prayer, more solemn chant.

I got up cautiously but I was no longer in the least dizzy, though my limbs still felt heavy. I went to the window to breathe in the evening air. A fresh jug of water had been placed on the table and I drank a glass of it with as much relish as I had ever drunk a glass of fine wine.

I watched the sky darken and the stars grow brighter. I wondered if I could find my way outside. I felt like walking at least a little way, but as I was thinking of it I heard quick footsteps and the Guest Master tapped and came in, smiling. He was a man whose face seemed to be set in a permanent beam of welcome and good spirits.

"Ah, Monsieur Snow, bonsoir, bonsoir. It is good. I came in and each time . . ." He made a gesture of sleep, closing his eyes, with his hands to the side of his head.

"Thank you, yes. I slept like a newborn."

"And so, you seem well again, but the Infirmarian will come again once more to be sure."

"No, I'm fine. Please don't trouble the father again. Is it too late for my meeting with the Librarian?"

"Ah, I fear yes. But he will be pleased to meet with you tomorrow morning. I did not wake you. It was better."

"I was wondering if I could take a short walk outside? I feel I need some fresh air."

"Ah. Now, let me see. I have the office soon, but yes,

come with me, come with me, take a little air—it is very mild. I will come to fetch you inside after the office and then it will be bringing your supper. We retire to bed early you see, and then tomorrow you will eat in the refectory with us, our guest. Please." He held open the door for me and we went out of the room and down the corridor.

The stone staircase led into a long, cool cloister and as we walked down it I heard the sound of footsteps coming from all sides, soft, quick, pattering on the stone, and then the monks appeared, hoods up, heads bowed, arms folded within the wide sleeves of their habits.

But the Guest Master led me out of a door at the far end of the cloister and into a wide courtyard under the stars. He pointed to a door in the wall.

"There, please, walk out of there and into the cloister garden. You will find it so still and pleasant. I will return for you in twenty minutes. Tomorrow, you see, you will find it easy to make your own way about."

He beamed and turned back, going quickly after the other monks toward the chapel, from where the bell continued to toll.

Twelve

I walked between the monastery buildings toward the cloister at the far end. No one was here save a scraggy little black and white cat which streaked away into the shadows on my approach. I looked with pleasure at the beauty of the pattern made by the line of arches and at the stones of the floor. There was no sound. The singing of the monks at their office was contained somewhere deep within the walls. At the end of the cloister, I stepped off the path and onto closely cut grass. I had found myself in the garden, though one without any flowerbeds or trees. I stopped. I was surrounded by cloisters on three sides, on the fourth by another building. There was moonlight enough to see by.

I wondered what kind of men came here to stay not for a few days' retreat or refreshment, but for life. Unusual men, it might seem. Yet the Guest Master was robust and energetic, a man you might meet anywhere.

I wondered how I would find the Librarian and the Abbot. And as I did so, I began to cross the grass. It was as I reached the center of the large rectangular garden that I noticed the pool. It too was rectangular, with wide stone surrounds and set level with the ground. I wondered if there were fish living a cool mysterious life in its depths.

It was as I drew close to it and looked down that I felt the small hand holding mine. I thought my heart would stop. But this time the hand did not clutch mine and there was no sense that I was being pulled forward. It was, as on that first evening, merely a child's hand in mine.

I looked down into the still, dark water on which the moonlight rested and as I looked I saw. What I saw was so clear and so strange and so real that I could not doubt it then, as I have never doubted it since.

I saw the face of a child in the water. It was upturned to look directly at me. There was no distortion from the water, it was not the moonlight playing tricks with the shadows. Everything was so still that there was not the slightest ripple to disturb the surface. It was not easy to guess at his age but he was perhaps three or four. He had a solemn and very beautiful face and the curls of his hair framed it. His eyes were wide open. It was not a dead face, this was a living, breathing child, though I saw no limbs or body, only the face. I looked into his eyes and he looked back into mine, and as we looked the grip of the small hand tightened. I could hardly breathe. The child's eyes had a particular expression. They were beseeching me, urging me. I closed my eyes. When I opened them, he was still there.

Now the small hand was tightening in mine and I felt the dreadful pull I had experienced before to throw myself forward into the water. I could not look at the child's face, because I knew that I would be unable to refuse what he wanted. His expression was one of such longing and need that I could never hold out against him. I closed my eyes, but then the pull of the hand became so strong that I was terrified of losing my balance. I felt both afraid and unwell, my heart pounding and my limbs weak so that, as I turned away from the pool, using every last ounce of determination, I stumbled and fell forward. As I did so, I reached my left hand across and tried to prize the grasp of the small fingers away, but there was nothing to take hold of, though the sensation of being held by them did not lessen.

"Leave me alone," I said. "Please go. Please go." I heard myself speak but my voice sounded odd, a harsh whispered cry as I struggled to control my breathing.

The hand still tugged mine, urging me to stand up, urging me to do what it wanted me to do, go where it wanted me to go.

"Let me go!" I shouted, and my shout echoed out into the silent cloisters.

I heard an exclamation and a hurried movement toward me across the grass and Frère Jean-Marc was kneeling beside me, taking me by the shoulders and lifting me easily into a sitting position, tutting in a gentle voice and telling me to be calm.

After a moment, my breathing slowed and I stopped shaking. A slight breeze came from the mountain, cool on my face, smelling of the pine trees.

"Tell me," the monk said, his face full of concern, "tell me what is troubling to you. Tell me—what is it that is making you afraid?"

Thirteen

There could have been no place more calming to the senses or enriching to the spirit than the great library at the monastery of Saint Mathieu.

Sitting there the next day in that quiet and beautiful space, I counted myself one of the most fortunate men on earth, and nothing that had happened to me seemed to be more than the brush of a gnat against my skin.

The library was housed in a three-story building separate from the rest, with a spiral stone staircase leading from the cloisters firstly into a simple reading room set with pale wooden desks, then up to the one holding, so the Librarian told me, all the sacred books and manuscripts, many of them in multiple copies. But it was the topmost room, with its tall, narrow windows letting in lances of clear light and with a gallery all the way round, which took my breath away. If I could compare it to any other library I knew, it would be to the Bodleian's Duke

Humfrey, that awe-inspiring space, but the monastery library was more spacious and without any claustrophobic feel.

At first, I had simply stood and gazed round me at the magnificence of the shelving, the solemnity of the huge collection, the order and symmetry of the great room. If the books had all been empty boxes it would still have been mightily impressive. There were slender stone pillars and recessed reading desks in the arched spaces between them.

The floor was of polished honey-colored wood and there was a central row of tables. At the far end, behind a carved wooden screen, was the office of the Librarian. Along the opposite end were tall cupboards which contained, I was told, the most precious manuscripts in the collection.

The cupboards were not locked. When I noted this, the Librarian simply smiled. "Mais pourquoi?"

Indeed. Where else in the world would so many rare and precious items be entirely safe from theft? The only reason they were kept out of sight was to protect them from damage.

⌒

THE LIBRARIAN HAD brought me book after wonderful book, simply for my delight—illuminated manuscripts, rare psalters, Bibles with magnificent bindings. He was an old man, rather bent, and he moved, as I had noticed all the monks moved, at a slow and measured pace, as if rush and hurry were not only wasteful of energy but unspiritual. Everything was accomplished but no one hurried. His English was almost flawless—he told me that he had spent five years studying at St. John's College, Cambridge—and his interest and learning were wide, his pleasure in the library clear to see. He had a special dispensation to speak to me, but he did not waste a word any more than he wasted a movement.

I had slept well and dreamlessly after a late visit from the Infirmarian, who had given me what he described as "un peu de somnifère gentil"—a dark green liquid in a medicine glass. He had checked me over and seemed satisfied that I was not physically ill. Frère Jean-Marc had brought my breakfast and explained that the Abbot had been spoken to and would like to see me at two o'clock but that he felt a visit to the library would be the best medicine. He was right.

"And now," the Librarian, Dom Martin, had said, coming toward the reading desk at which I was sitting in one of the alcoves.

From there, I could look into the body of the library, and the sunshine making a few lozenges of brightness on the wooden floor. The place smelled as all such places do, of paper and leather, polish and age and wisdom—a powerful intoxicant to anyone whose life is bound up, as mine had long been, with books.

"Here it is. Perhaps you have seen one of these before—there are over two hundred in the world, after all—but you will not have seen this particular one. I think you are about to have a wonderful surprise." He smiled, his old face full of a sort of teasing delight as he held the book in his hands.

I had indeed seen a Shakespeare First Folio before. As he said, it is not particularly rare and I had looked closely at several both in England and abroad. I had also spent some time before coming to Saint Mathieu checking two existing Folios, so that I would be able to judge whether what I was to be shown was genuine. It was not impossible. The whereabouts of only a couple of hundred copies are known now, but the book would have had a printing of perhaps 750. Even if most of those did not survive, there was nothing to say several might not still remain, buried in some library—possibly, a library such as this one.

The book Dom Martin held in his outstretched hands was large. He laid it down with care on the desk before me but he did not wait for me to examine it. One of the innumerable bells was ringing, summoning him away to prayer. He walked out of the great room and I heard his footsteps going away down the stone staircase as the bell continued to toll. Two other monks, who had been at some quiet work, followed him and I was left alone to examine what I knew within a few moments to be, with precious little doubt, a very fine copy of the First Folio. That in itself was exciting enough, but in addition, on the title page, the book bore the signature of Ben Jonson. Of course I would need to check, but from memory I was sure the signature was right. So this, then, was his copy of Shakespeare that I held in my hands. It was a remarkable moment.

I spent some time turning the pages carefully, reveling in the book and hoping that I might manage to procure it for Sir Edgar Merriman. After a moment, I looked up and around that handsome room. I felt well. I felt quite calm. I also felt safe, as I no longer felt truly safe anywhere outside, for fear of what might happen and of feeling the small hand creeping into mine. I steered my attention quickly back to the book before me.

I SPENT THE rest of the morning comfortably in the library before returning to my room at one o'clock, when the Guest Master brought my simple food. At two he returned to escort me to the Abbot. I had not left the building since the previous night, though I could see that it was a beautiful day and the bright sky and clear air ought to tempt me out. But whenever I so much as thought about venturing beyond the safety of the monastery walls, I felt a lurch of fear again.

THE ABBOT WAS unlike the figure I had imagined. I had expected a tall, imposing, solemn, older man. He was small, with a neat-featured face, deep-set eyes. He spoke good English, he listened carefully, he was rather expressionless but then his face would break into a warm, engaging smile. I warmed to him. I felt reassured by him and after ten minutes or so in his presence, I realized that he was a man with an unprepossessing exterior that concealed considerable human understanding and wisdom.

We talked business for a few moments in his tidy office, about the sale of the monastery's treasures and the Folio in particular, and I knew that things would probably be arranged smoothly. The deliberation about whether to sell anything at all had been long, careful and probably painful, but once the decision had been made, they would be quite pragmatic and arrange things efficiently. They had to ensure the upkeep and survival of the monastery for the future.

"Monsieur Snow, I would like you to feel you may stay with us here until you feel quite well again. We will look after you, of course. This is a very healing place."

"I know. I feel that very much. And I am very grateful to you."

He waited quietly, patiently, and as he waited I felt an urge to tell him, tell him everything that had happened, recount the strange events and my own terrors, ask him—for what? To believe me? To explain?

There was no sound in the room. I wondered what the monks were doing now and presumed they were in their own cells, praying, reading holy books, meditating. From far on the mountainside came the tinkle of the cowbells. I looked at the Abbot.

"I wonder," I said, "if I am going mad or being persecuted in some way. I only know that things keep happening to me which I do not understand. I have always been a healthy man and quite serene. Until—this began."

His eyes were steady on my face, his hands still, rest-

ing on either side of his chair. His habit, with the hood
back, lay in perfect folds, as if they had been painted by
an old master. He did not urge me. I felt that he would
accept whatever I chose to do—leave the room now,
without saying more, or confide in him and ask for his
counsel.

I began to talk. Perhaps I had not intended to tell him
everything, even the details of my brother's own breakdown, but I found myself doing so. Once, he got up and
poured me a glass of water from a carafe on the stone
ledge. I drank it eagerly before continuing. The sunlight,
which had been slanting across his desk, moved round
and away. Twice the bell rang, but the Abbot took no
notice of it, merely sat in his chair, his eyes on me, his
expression full of concern, listening, listening.

I finished speaking and fell silent, suddenly drained of
every gram of energy. I knew that when I returned to the
guest room I would sleep another of the deep, exhausted
sleeps I had grown used to having in this place.

The Abbot sat thoughtfully for some moments as
I leaned back, slightly dizzy but in some way washed
clean and clear, as if I had confessed a catalogue of terrible sins to the priest.

At last I said, "You think I am mad."

He waved his hand dismissively. "Mais non. I think
terrible things have happened to you and you are pro-
foundly affected by them. But what things and why?
Can you tell me—nothing like this has ever happened
in your life until the first visit to this house entirely by
chance?"

"Absolutely nothing. Of that I'm quite certain."

"And this hand? This hand of the child at first did not seem in any way upsetting?"

"No. It seemed very strange."

"Bien sûr."

"But it was not until later that I felt any hostility, any desire to do me harm. Real harm. To lead me into harm."

"Into these pools. Into the water. Over the precipice into the lake of the gorge."

"But why?" I cried out loudly. "Why does this thing want to do me harm?"

"I think that either you can choose never to know that and simply pray that in time it will be tired of failure and abandon this quest. Or you can choose to find out, if that shall be possible, and so . . ."

"To lay the ghost."

"Oui."

"Do you believe this thing—child—whatever it is—do you believe it truly exists?"

"Spirits exist, bien sûr. Good exists. Evil exists. Perhaps the spirit of a child is disturbed and unhappy. Perhaps it has a need." He shrugged. "I do think you have suffered. I think you will do well to remain here and let us help you, refresh you."

"But here of all places, surely, this should not have happened again? If I am not safe here . . ."

"You are entirely safe here. Do not doubt it. You will be given all the strength, all the protection of our Blessed Lord and his saints, and of our prayers for you. You are surrounded by strong walls of prayer, Monsieur Snow. Do not forget."

"Thank you. I will try."

"This evening, if you feel well and able, join us in the chapel for our night prayers. These give great peace, great power to combat the perils of the darkness. And if you decide to confront le fantôme, and your terrors, then you will also be under protection, under the shield of our prayers."

"What do you honestly think I should do, Father?"

"Ah. For me, everything is the better when faced. You draw the sting. But you only can make this choice."

He stood in one graceful, flowing movement of body and robes together and held up his right hand to make the sign of the cross over me, then led me toward the door. As I left, he stood watching me walk down the cloister and I glanced back, to see that his expression was grave. He had believed me. He had listened attentively and dismissed nothing, nor tried to explain any of it away. For that I was deeply grateful.

～

I RETURNED TO my room and slept, but when I woke I longed for outside air and found my way, with only a couple of wrong turnings down stone corridors, to the courtyard. This time, I walked in the opposite direction from the one I had taken the previous night and went instead through the gate in the wall to the main entrance and, from there, headed toward the pine-covered slopes and a narrow path that climbed steeply and would, I was sure, eventually lead to the top of one of the peaks. I am no mountaineer. I walked for perhaps twenty minutes along the narrow path that wound between the great, dark trees. The ground was soft with a carpet of pine needles, my feet made no sound and when I looked up I could see violet-blue patches of sky far above the tree-tops. I came to a clearing where two or three trees had been felled and were lying on the ground. I sat down. There was no birdsong, no animal movement, but tiny spiders and other insects scurried about on the logs and at my feet. I realized that I was waiting. I even held out my hand.

One of the small spiders ran across it. Nothing more.

I MADE MY way carefully back down the path. But when I went through the gate I heard voices coming not from inside the monastery but from somewhere beyond the outer courtyard. I found my way through the cloisters until I approached the inner garden. A group of about a dozen of the monks were standing around the pool. One held a thurible which he was swinging gently, sending soft clouds of incense drifting across the surface of the water. Another carried a cross. The rest were singing a plainchant, holding their books in front of them, heads slightly bowed. I stood still until the singing died away and then saw the Abbot lift his hand and give a final blessing while making the sign of the cross. I realized that the pool in which I had seen the upturned face of the child and toward which I had been so urgently drawn was being blessed, made holy. Made safe.

I was glad of it. But as I slipped back through the cloisters, I knew that the Abbot's precaution had not been necessary, for it was not the monks who were in danger, or indeed any other person who might visit this quiet and holy place. Whatever it was that had come here had come because of me. When I left, it would leave too. Leave with me.

Fourteen

Four Ragged Staff Lane
Oxford OX2 1ZZ

Adam,

Terrific news. Well done! I was sure you and the monks would see eye to eye and am delighted you confirmed that it was indeed a First Folio and managed to secure it. Lucky client.

Come to Oxford again soon.

Best,
Fergus

Ravenhead
Ditchforth
West Sussex

Dear Mr. Snow

We are greatly looking forward to seeing you here on Wednesday next, to dine and sleep and tell us about your visit to France. My husband is on tenterhooks.

Meanwhile, having more time on my hands as I grow old than perhaps I should, I have been delving a little into the story of the White House and have turned up one or two snippets of information which can perhaps be pieced together. But it may no longer be of the slightest interest to you and of course you must tell me if that is the case.

We will expect you somewhere between five and six o'clock.

With every good wish
Alice Merriman

Hello. This is Adam Snow. I am sorry I am not available. Please leave me a message and I will return your call.

It's Hugo. Not sure if you're back. I've been thinking about what you told me when you came up here last time. I just wanted to say I'm sure it's nothing. Maybe you had a virus. You know, people get depression after flu, that sort of stuff. So, if you're worried about it, well, don't be. I'm sure it was nothing. OK, that's it. Give us a call some time.

Fifteen

Of course I had to return. As soon as I had arranged to go down and see Sir Edgar Merriman about the Folio, I became aware of the sensation. It was like a magnetic pull upon my whole being. It was there when I slept and when I woke, it was there at the back of my mind all day and it was there even within my dreams. I could not have resisted whatever force it was and I did not try. I was afraid of it and I think I knew now that the best, the only thing to do if I was to retain my sanity was to obey. I hoped that the monks were continuing to pray for my protection.

This time I did not get lost. This time I did not come upon it by chance. This time I had marked my journey out on a map a couple of days before and gone carefully over the last few miles, so that I knew exactly where I was going and how long it would take me from when I left the A road. This time I drove slowly down the lane, between the high banks, the elephantine tree trunks pressing in on me in the gloom, and I was aware of everything as if I had taken some mind-expanding drug, so clearly did I see it all, so vivid the detail of every last tree root and clump of earth and overhanging branch seem.

It was a tranquil day but with a cloudy sky. Earlier there had been a couple of showers and by the time I got out of the car in the clearing the air was humid and still.

I had come prepared. I had bought a pair of wire cutters and some secateurs. I was not going to let undergrowth or fences keep me out.

What would I find? I did not know and I tried not to give my imagination any rein. I would obey the insistent, silent voice that told me I must go back and once there I would see. I would see.

❧

EVERYTHING SEEMED AS before. I stood for a moment beside the car and then went to the gate and pushed it open, feeling it scrape along the ground just as on my previous visit, and walked toward the old ticket booth. The notice still hung there, the grille was still down. I stood and waited for a moment. In my left hand I carried the cutters, my right held nothing. But after several minutes nothing had happened. My hand remained empty. In a gesture that was half deliberate, half a reflex, I curled my fingers. There was no response.

❧

THE AIR WAS heavy, the bushes on either side lush, the leaves of some ancient laurel glistening with moisture from the earlier rain. I had put on wellington boots, so that I could push my way through the long grass without inconvenience.

I came out into the clearing. There was the house. The White House. Empty. Half derelict, the glass broken in one or two of the windows. The stones of the courtyard in front of it were thick with pads of velvety moss.

I turned away. To the side was another low wooden gate. It had an old padlock and rusty chain across it and both gleamed with moisture. But the padlock hung open and the gate was so rotten it gave at once to my hand and I went through. Ahead of me was a path leading between some ancient high yew hedges. I followed it. I could see quite well because although the sky was overcast it was barely half past five and there was plenty of light left. The path led straight. At the end, an archway was cut into the hedge and although ivy trailed down over it, the way was clear and I had no need of the cutters I had brought. I went through and down four steps made of brick and set in a semicircle, then found that I had come out into what had clearly once been a huge lawn with a high wall at the far end and the thickly overgrown remains of wide flower borders. There were fruit trees, gnarled and pitted old apples and pears, forming a sort of avenue—I know there are proper gardening terms for these things. On the far side of the lawn, whose grass was so high that it came over the tops of my boots and was mixed with nettles and huge vicious thistles, there ran yet another tall yew hedge in which was another arch. I turned round. To one side a path led diagonally toward woodland. I went in the opposite direction, to an open gate in a high wall. On the other side of it I found what seemed to have been an area of patterned beds set formally between old gravel paths. I remembered pictures of Elizabethan knot gardens. There were small trees planted in the center of each bed, though most of them looked dead. I leaned over and picked a wiry stem from a bush beside me, breaking it between my fingers. It was lavender.

Every so often, I paused and waited. But there was nothing. Nothing stirred and no birds sang.

IT WAS A SAD place, but I did not feel uneasy or afraid in any way, there seemed to be nothing odd about this abandoned garden. I felt melancholy. It had once been a place of color and beauty, full of growth and variety—full of people. I looked around me, trying to imagine them strolling about, bending over to look more closely at a flower, admiring, enjoying, in pairs or small groups.

Now there was no one and nature was taking everything back to itself. In a few more years would there be anything left to say there had been a garden here at all?

The silence was extraordinary, the same sort of silence I had experienced in the grounds of the monastery. But here there were no gentle cowbells reassuring me from the near distance. I wondered which way to go. I had come because I had had no choice. But what next?

As if in reply, the small hand crept into mine and held it fast and I felt myself pulled forward through the long grass toward the far hedge.

THE SOFT SWISHING sound my boots made as I walked broke the oppressive stillness. Once I thought I heard something else, just behind me, and swung round. There was nothing. Perhaps a rabbit or a stray cat was following—I was going to say "us," for that was unmistakably how I felt now. There were two of us.

I reached the far side and the arch in the high dark yew and stopped just inside it. Looking ahead, I could see that I was about to enter another garden, a sunken garden that was approached down the flight of a dozen steps at my feet, semicircular again and broken here and there, with weeds growing between the cracks. On the far side stood a vast cedar tree. A very overgrown gravel path ran all the way round. It was not a large enclosure and the surrounding yew hedge closed in like high, dark walls. Because of these and the trees on the other side, less light came in here than into the wide open space I had just left, and so the grass in the center had not grown wild but was still short, something like a lawn, though spoiled by yellowish weed and with bald patches here and there, where the earth or stones showed through, like the skull through an old person's thinning hair.

I did not want to step down into it. I felt that if I did I would be suffocated between these dark hedges. But the small hand was holding mine tightly and trying with everything in its power to get me to move.

And then, as I looked down, I noticed something else. In the center was a strange circle, like a fairy ring. I could only just make it out, for it seemed to be marked from nothing in particular—a darker line of grass perhaps, or small stones concealed below the surface. I stared at it and it seemed not to be there.

The grey clouds above me parted for a moment and a dilute and watery sun struggled through for a moment and in that moment the circle appeared quite clearly against a fleeting brightness.

THE SMALL HAND was grasping mine in desperation now. It was as if someone was in danger of falling over the edge of a cliff and clutching at me for dear life, but at the same time it was trying to pull me over with it. If it fell it would make sure that I would fall too. It was exactly the same as it had been on the edge of the preci-pice in the Vercors, except that that had been real. Here there was no cliff, merely a few steps. I still did not want to go down, but I could no longer resist the strength of the hand.

"All right," I said aloud, my voice sounding strange in that desolate place. "All right. I'll do what you want."

I went, being careful with my footing on the loose and cracked stones, until I was standing in the sunken garden, on the same level as the half-visible circle. But at that moment the sun went in and a sudden rush of wind blew, shifting the heavy branches of the great tree on the far side before it died away at once, leaving an eerie and total stillness.

"What are you doing here?"

The sound of the voice was like a shot in the back. I have never felt such a split second of absolute shock and terror.

"The garden is no longer open to the public."

I turned.

SHE WAS STANDING at the top of the steps inside the archway, looking down, staring at me out of a face devoid of expression, and yet she gave off an air of hostility to me, of threat. She was old, though I could not guess, as one often can, exactly how old, but her face was a mesh of fine wrinkles and those do not come at sixty. Her hair was very thin and scraped back into some sort of comb and she seemed to be bundled into layers of old clothes, random skirts and cardigans and an ancient bone-colored mackintosh, like a bag lady who preyed upon the rubbish sacks at the curbside.

I stammered an apology, said I had not realized anyone would be there, thought the place was derelict . . . I stumbled over my words because she had startled me and I felt somehow disoriented, which was perhaps because I was standing on a lower level, almost as if I were at her feet.

"Won't you come to the house?"

I stared at her.

"There is nothing here now. The garden has gone. But if you would like to see it as it was I would be glad to show you the pictures."

"As it was?"

But she was turning away, a small, wild figure in her bundled clothing, the wisps of ancient grey hair escaping at the back of her neck like skeins of cloud.

"Come to the house . . ." Her voice faded away as she disappeared back into the tangled grass and clumps of weed that was the garden on the other side.

For a moment I did not move. I could not move. I looked down at my feet, to where I had seen the strange circle in the ground, but it was not there now. It had been some optical illusion, then, a trick of the light. In any case, I had no idea what I had thought it represented—perhaps the foundations of an old building, a summer house, a gazebo? I stepped forward and scraped about with my foot. There was nothing. I tried to remember the stories we had learned as children about fairy rings. Then I turned away. Somewhere beyond the arch, she would be waiting for me. "Come to the house."

Half of me was curious, wanting to know who she was and what I would find in a house I had thought was abandoned and semi-derelict. But I was afraid too. I thought I might dive back through the undergrowth until I reached the gate and the drive, the safety of my car, ignore the old woman. Run away.

It was my choice.

I waded my way through the undergrowth beneath the gathering sky. It was airless and very still. The silence seemed palpable, like the silence that draws in around one before a storm.

It was only as I reached the path that led out of the gardens between overgrown shrubs and trees toward the gate that I realized I was alone. The old woman had vanished and the small hand was no longer grasping mine.

Sixteen

The key was in my trouser pocket. I had only to open the car doors, throw in the tools and get away from that place, but as I went I glanced quickly back over my shoulder at the house. The door was standing wide open where I was certain that it had previously been shut fast. I hesitated. I wanted to turn and head for the car but I was transfixed by sight of the door, sure that the old woman must have opened it because she was expecting me to enter, was waiting for me now somewhere inside.

"Are you there?" she called.

So I had no choice after all. I dropped the secateurs and cutters on the ground and went slowly toward the house, looking up as I did so at the windows whose frames were rotten, at the paint that was faded and peeled almost away, at the windowpanes which were filthy and broken here and there, and in a couple of the rooms actually boarded over. Surely no one could possibly live here. Surely this place was, as I had seen it at first, ruined and deserted.

I walked up the steps and hesitated at the open door. I could see nothing inside the house, no light, no movement.

"Hello?" My voice echoed down the dark corridor ahead.

There was no reply. No one was here. The wind had blown the door open. Yet the old woman had been in the garden. I had seen her and she had spoken to me. Then I heard a sound, perhaps that of a voice. I took a step inside.

It was several moments before my eyes grew used to the darkness, but then I saw that I was standing in a hall and that a passageway led off to my right. I saw a glimmer of light at the far end. Then the voice again.

The house smelled of rot and mold and must. This could not possibly still be a home. It must not have been inhabited for decades. I put out my hand to touch the wall and then guide myself along the passage, though I was sure that I was being foolish and told myself to go back. I had only just regained my senses and a measure of calm since the awful things that had happened: in Oxford, in the mountains of the Vercors and the garden of the monastery. I was certain that those things were somehow connected with this house, and my first visit here, with the first time I had felt the small hand take hold of mine. Was I mad? I should not have come back and I certainly should not be going any further now.

But I was powerless to stop. I could not go back. I had to know.

Keeping my hand to the wall, which was cold and crumbled to the touch of my fingers here and there, I made my way with great caution down the passage in the direction of what, after a few yards, I thought was the light of candles.

"Please come in."

IT TOOK ME a few seconds to orient myself within one of the weirdest rooms I had ever entered. The wavering tallow light came not from candles after all, but from a couple of ancient paraffin lamps which gave off a strong smell. There was even a little daylight in the room too, filtering in through French windows at the back, but the glass was filthy, the creeper and overhanging greenery outside obscured much of it and it was impossible to tell if the sky was thundery and dark or whether it was simply occluded by the dirt.

It was a large room but whole recesses of it were in shadow and seemed to be full of furniture swathed in sheeting. Otherwise, it was as if I had entered the room in which the boy Pip had encountered Miss Havisham.

In one corner was a couch which seemed to be made up as a bed with a pile of cushions and an ancient quilt thrown over it. There was a wicker chair facing the French windows and a dresser with what must once have been a fine set of candelabra and rows of rather beautiful china, but the silver was tarnished and stained, the china and the dresser surface covered in layers of dust.

She was sitting at a large round table in the center of the room, on which one of the lamps stood, the old mackintosh hanging on her chair-back but the rest of her still huddled in the mess of ragged old clothes. Her scalp looked yellow in the oily light, which shone through the frail little pile of hair on top of her head.

"I must apologize," she said. "There are so few visitors now. People still remember the garden, you know, and occasionally they come here, but not many. It is all a long time ago. Look out there."

I followed her gaze, beyond the dirty windows to where I could make out a veranda, with swags of wisteria hanging down in uneven curtains, and another wicker chair.

"I can see the garden better from there. Won't you sit down?"

I hesitated. She leaned over and swept a pile of all manner of rubbish, including old newspapers, cardboard and bits of cloth, off a chair beside her.

"I will show you the pictures first," she said. "Then we can go round the garden."

I had had no idea that anyone could possibly be living here and now that I had found her I could not imagine how she did indeed "live," how she ate and if she ever left the place. She was clearly half mad, an ancient woman living in some realm of the past. I wondered if she belonged here, if she had been a housekeeper, or had just come upon it and broken in, a squatter among the debris and decay.

She looked up at me. Her eyes were watery and pale, like the eyes of most very old people, but there was something about the look in them that unnerved me. Her skin was powdery and paper-thin, her nose a bony hook. It was impossible to guess her age. And yet there was a strange beauty about her, a decaying, desiccated beauty, but it held my gaze for all that. She seemed to belong with those dried and faded flowers people used to press between pages, or with a bowl of old potpourri that exudes a faint, sweet, ghostly scent when it is disturbed. Yet when she spoke again her voice was clear and sharp, with an elegant pronunciation. Nothing about her added up.

"I think you've visited the garden before Mr. . . ."

"No. I got lost down the lane leading to the house one evening a few months ago. I'd never heard of the garden. And my name is Snow."

She was looking at me with an odd, quizzical half-smile.

"Do please sit down. I said I would show you the albums. People sometimes come for that, you know, as well as those who expect the garden still to be open and everything just as it was." She looked up at me. "But nothing is ever just as it was, is it, Mr. Snow?"

"I don't think I caught your name."

"I presumed you knew." She went on looking at me for a second or two, before pulling a large leather-bound album toward her from several on the table. The light in the room was eerie, a strange mixture of the flickering oil lamp and the grey evening seeping in from outside, filtered through the overhanging creeper.

"You really cannot look at these standing up. But perhaps I can get you something? It is rather too late for tea. I could offer you sherry."

"Thank you. No. I really have to leave, I'm afraid. I'm on my way to stay with friends—I still have some miles to drive. I should have left . . ."

I heard myself babbling on. She sat quite still, her hand on the album, as if waiting patiently for my voice to splutter and die before continuing.

For a second the room was absolutely silent and we two frozen in it, neither of us speaking, neither moving, and as if something odd had happened to time.

I knew that I could not leave. Something was keeping me here, partly but not entirely against my will, and I was calmly sure that if I tried to go I would be detained, either by the old woman's voice or by the small hand, which for the moment at least was not resting in mine. But if I tried to escape, it would be there, gripping tightly, holding me back.

I pulled out a chair and sat down, a little apart from her, at the dark oak table, whose surface was smeared with layers of dirt and dust.

She glanced at me and I saw it again, the strange beauty shining through age and decay, yellowing teeth and desiccated skin and dry wisps of old hair.

"This was the house when I first found it. And the garden. Not very good photographs. Little box cameras."

She shook her head and turned the page.

"The wilderness," she said, looking down. "That's what the children said when we first came here. I remember so well—Margaret rushing round the side of the house and looking at it—the huge trees, weeds taller than she was, rhododendrons . . ." She lifted her hand above her head. "She stopped there. Look, just there. Michael came racing after her and they stood together and she shouted, 'It's our wilderness!'"

She rested her hand on the photograph and was silent for a moment. I could see the pictures, tanned with age and rather small. But it was all familiar, because it was all the same as today. The wilderness had grown back, the house was as dilapidated as it had been all those years ago. All those years? How many? How old was she?

"You!" I said suddenly. "You are Denisa Parsons. It was your garden."

"Of course," she said dismissively. "Who did you think I was?"

My head swam suddenly and the table seemed to pitch forward in front of me. I reached out my hand to grab hold of it.

She was smiling vaguely down at the album and now she began to turn the pages one after the other, making an occasional remark. "The builders . . . look . . . digging out the ground . . . trees coming down . . . light . . . so much light suddenly."

The flicking of the pages confused me. I felt nauseated. The smell of the paraffin was sickening, the room fetid. There was another smell. I supposed it was accumulated dirt and decay.

"I'm trying to find it." Flick. Flick. "Margaret never forgave me. Nor Michael, but Michael was more stoical, I suppose. And then of course he went away. But Margaret. It was hate. Bitter hate. You see"—she rested her hand on the table and stared down, as if reading something there—"I sent them away to boarding school. When we first came here, after Arthur died, it never occurred to me that I would want them out of the way. He had left me the money, enough to buy somewhere else, and I had never liked the suburbs. But when we came here something happened. I had to do it, you see, I had to pull it all down and make something magnificent of my own. And they were in the way."

She turned a page, then another.

"Here it is, you see. Here it all is. The past is here. Look . . . the Queen came. Here she is. There were pieces in all the newspapers. Look."

But I could not look, for she was turning the pages too quickly, and when she had got to the end of the book, she reached for another.

"I have to go," I said. "I have to be somewhere else."

She ignored me.

I stood up and pushed back my chair. The room seemed to be closing in on us, shrinking to the small area round the table, lit by the oily lamplight.

I almost pitched forward. I felt nauseous and dizzy.

And then she let out an odd laugh. "Here," she said. "This one. Look here."

She turned the album round so that I could see it. There were four photographs on the left and two on the right-hand side, all of them cut from newspapers and somewhat faded.

They seemed to be of various parts of the White House garden as it had been—the yew hedge was visible in one, a series of interlinked rose arches in another. There were groups of visitors strolling across a lawn. The one she pointed to seemed to be of a broad terrace on which benches were placed in front of a stone balustrade. Several large urns were spilling over with flowers. It was just possible to see steps leading down, presumably to a lower level and another part of the garden.

She was not pointing to the book. She was sitting back in her chair and seemed to be looking into some far distance, almost unaware of where she was or of my presence. She was so totally still that I wondered for a second if she was still breathing.

And then, because now it was what I had to do, I could not turn my eyes away, I looked down at the page of photographs, and then, bending my head to see it more closely, to the one on the right at which she had pointed. There was a caption—I do not remember what it read but it was of no consequence, perhaps "A sunny afternoon" or "Visitors enjoying the garden." I saw that the cutting was from a magazine and that it seemed to be part of a longer feature, with several double columns and another smaller picture. But it was not the writing, it was not the headline at which I was staring.

The black-and-white photograph of the terrace

showed a couple beside one of the benches and seated on the bench in a row were some children. Three boys. Neat, open-necked white shirts. Grey trousers. White socks. Sandals. One wore a sleeveless pullover knitted in what looked like Fair Isle. I looked at it more closely and, as I did so, I had a strange feeling of familiarity, as if I knew the pullover. And then I realized that it was not only the pullover which was familiar. I knew the boy. I knew him because he was myself, aged perhaps five years old. I remembered the pullover because it had been mine. I could see the colors: fawn, pale blue, brown.

I was the boy in the pullover and the one sitting next to me was my brother, Hugo.

But who the other boy was, the boy who sat at the end of our row and who was younger than either of us, I had no idea. I did not remember him.

"Come outside," she was saying now. "Let me show you."

Yes. I needed to be outside, to be anywhere in the fresh air and away from the house and that room with its smell, and the yellowing light. I followed her, thinking that, whatever happened, I had the key to the car in my pocket, I could get in and go within a few moments. But she was not leaving the room by the open door into the dark corridor, she had gone across to the French windows and turned the key. Yet surely these glass doors could not have been opened for years. The creeper was twined thick as rope around the joints and hinges.

They opened easily, as such a door would in a dream, and she brushed aside the heavy curtain of greenery as if it were so many overhanging cobwebs and I stepped out after her onto the wide veranda. It was twilight but the sky had cleared of the earlier, heavy cloud.

I remember that she turned her head and that she looked at me as I stood behind her. I remember her expression. I remember her eyes. I remember the way the old clothes she wore bunched up under the ancient mac when we had been inside the house.

I remember those things and I have clung on to the memory because it is—was—real, I saw those things, I was there. I could feel the evening air on my face. This was not a dream.

Yet everything that happened next had a quite different quality. It was real, it was happening, I was there. Yet it was not. I was not.

I despair. I am confused. I do not know how to describe what I felt, though in part the simple word "unwell" would suffice. My legs were unsteady, my heart raced and I had seconds of dizziness followed by a sudden small jolt, like an electric shock, as if I had somehow come back into myself.

❧

AS WE LEFT the shadow of the house and went down the stone steps, the evening seemed to retreat—the sun was still out after all and the air was less cold. I supposed heavy clouds had made it seem later and darker and now those were clearing, giving us a soft and slightly pearlescent end to the day.

Denisa Parsons stayed a few paces ahead of me and, as we walked, I saw that we must have come out onto a different side of the garden, one which I had not seen before and not even guessed about, a part that was still carefully tended—still a garden and not a jungle. The grass was mown, the paths were graveled and without weeds and a wide border against a high stone wall still flowered with late roses among the green shrubs. I looked around, trying to get my bearings. I still felt unsteady. A squirrel sprang from branch to branch of a huge cedar tree to my right, making me start, but the old woman did not seem to notice, she simply walked on, and her walk was quite steady and purposeful, not faltering or cautious as I would have expected.

"I had no idea you kept up some of the garden like this," I said. "I thought it had all gone back to nature. You must have plenty of help."

She did not reply, only went on, a few steps ahead of me, neither turning her head again nor giving any sign that she had registered my words. We went down a gravel path which was in heavy shade, toward a yew hedge I thought looked familiar—but all high, dark green hedges look alike to me and there was nothing to distinguish it. The grass was mown short but there were no more flowerbeds and, as we continued on the same, rather monotonous way, I thought that maintenance must probably be done by some outside contractor who came in once a week to mow and trim hedges. A couple of times a year he might spray the gravel to get rid of weeds. What else was there to do?

The shade was reaching across the grass like fingers grasping at the last of the sunlight. And then she turned.

We had reached the arch in the yew hedge and were at the top of the flight of stone steps, looking down to where I had seen the sunken garden, overgrown and wild, its stone paths broken and weed-infested. Below me had been the strange circle, like a shading in the grass, which had been there and then not there, an optical illusion, perhaps caused by a cloud moving in front of the sun.

But what I saw ahead was not a wilderness. It certainly seemed to be the same sunken garden, reminding me of somewhere Italian I must once have visited, but it was immaculately ordered, with low hedges outlining squares and rectangles that contained beds of what I recognized as herbs, very regularly arranged. There were raked gravel paths and, on the far side, another flight of steps leading up to some sort of small stone temple.

And then I glanced down. At my feet was not some shadowy outline, like a great fairy-ring, but a pool, a still, dark pool set flat into the grass and with a stone rim, and I saw that, as this was a very formal garden of careful symmetry, its exact counterpart was on the opposite side. In between them stood a stone circle on which was an elaborate sundial painted in enameled gold and blue.

But it was the pool into which I stared now, the pool with its few thick, motionless, flowerless lily pads and its slow, silent fish moving about heavily under the surface of the water.

I turned to Denisa Parsons to ask for an explanation, but as I did so two things happened very quickly.

The small hand had crept into mine and begun to pull me forward with a tremendous, terrifying strength and, as it did so, a voice spoke my name. It was a real voice, and I seemed to know whose voice it was, yet it sounded different, distorted in some way.

It was whispering my name over and over again and the whisper grew louder and clearer and more urgent. On every previous occasion, whoever the owner of the small hand might be, that person had always been completely silent. I had never heard the faintest whisper on the air. But now I heard something quite clearly.

"Adam!" it said. "Adam. Adam. Adam." Then silence, and my name again, the cry growing a little louder and more urgent. "Adam. Adam." At the same time, the small hand was pulling me so hard I lost my balance and half fell down the steps, and went stumbling after it, or with it, as it dragged me toward the pool.

I closed my eyes, fearful of what was there, what I knew that I should see, as I had seen it in the pool at the monastery.

"Here. Here. Here."

I flung my right arm up into the air to shake off the grip of the small hand and, as I did so, looked toward the archway in some sort of desperate plea to the old woman to help me.

She was not there. The arch in the hedge was hollow, with only darkness, like a blank window, behind.

I DO NOT know if I cried out, I do not remember if the hand still clung to mine. I do not know anything, other than that the voice was still in my ears but wavering and becoming fainter and slightly distorted as the world tumbled in upon me and I felt myself fall, and not onto the hard ground but into a bottomless, swirling, dark vortex that had opened up at my feet.

Seventeen

I am sure that for a few minutes I must have been unconscious, before I felt myself surfacing, as if I had been diving in deep water and was slowly coming to the light and air. But the air felt close and damp and there was very little light. How long had I been at the house? I had gone there in daylight, now it was almost dark.

I was lying on the ground. I reached out my hand and felt cold stone and something rough. Gravel. Gradually, my head cleared and I found that I could sit up. It took me several minutes to remember where I was. The garden was dark, but when my eyes adjusted to it I could see a little.

I seemed to be unhurt, although I was dazed. Had I fainted? Had I tripped and fallen and perhaps knocked myself out? No, because I would surely have felt pain somewhere and there was none.

I was alone. The garden was still. The bushes and trees around me did not rustle or stir. No bird called.

I waited until fragments of recollection floated nearer to me and began to form clearer shapes in my mind. The old woman in the strange bundled clothing. The room in which she lived in squalor, deep in the near-derelict house. Their smell. The wavering sound of her voice. The garden.

That part of the garden she had led me into which was not overgrown and neglected, but mown and tidy, with lawn and trees, shrubs and flowerbeds, arches in the high hedge leading down neat flights of steps to . . .

I got carefully to my feet.

I saw the dark gleaming surface of the pool, the flat stone ledge that ran round it.

Golden fish gliding beneath the surface.

A bench.

Had there been a bench?

Bench. Bench.

My legs gave way beneath me again and I felt a wave of nausea. Bile rose into my mouth and I retched onto the cold ground.

AND THEN I heard something, some ordinary and reassuringly familiar sound. The sound of a car. I wiped my mouth on the back of my hand.

I could not get up again and for a while everything was dark and silent, but after a moment I saw a light flash somewhere, dip away, flash again, and a few moments later heard something else, the sound of someone pushing through the undergrowth. And calling out.

"Mr. Snow? Mr. Snow?"

I tried to reply but made only an odd, strangled sound in my throat.

The light sliced across the grass behind me.

"Mr. Snow?"

I did not recognize the voice.

"Are you there? Mr. Snow?"

And then someone almost tripped over me and the beam of a large torch was shining into my face and the man was bending down to me, murmuring with surprise and concern.

I closed my eyes in overwhelming relief.

Eighteen

I lay awake for a long time that night. I had been given a stiff whisky on arriving at the Merrimans' and then encouraged to have a hot bath. Lady Merriman was anxious for me to stay in bed and be given supper on a tray, but I wanted to get back to normality by eating with them, talking, giving all my news about the First Folio, so that I would not have to spend time alone going over what had—or had not—happened. I was quickly restored by the good malt and deep hot water and felt no after-effects of my having—what? Tripped and fallen, knocking myself out? Fainted? I had no idea and preferred not to speculate, but certainly I was not injured in any way, apart from having a sore bruise on my elbow where it had hit the ground under my weight.

Lady Merriman said little but I knew that her sharp blue eyes missed nothing and that, in spite of her usual quiet reserve, she was the one who had raised the alarm and who had guessed where I might be found when I failed to arrive at the house.

She told me that the police had been called first, but that there were no reports of road accidents.

"Then I had a sixth sense, you know," she said. "And that has never let me down. I knew you were there. I hope you don't think that weird in any way, Mr. Snow. I am not a witch. But people don't always like it if you mention things of this sort. I have learned to stay silent."

"I am very grateful for your sixth sense," I said. "Nor do I find it in the least weird. A lot of people have a slightly telepathic side to them . . . I am inclined to think it fairly normal. My mother often knew when a letter would arrive from someone, even if she was not expecting it and indeed hadn't heard from that person for years."

"My husband is skeptical, but you know, after all this time even he has learned not to argue with my instincts. It doesn't often happen but when it does . . ."

"Well, thank God it did today. I might have been lying there all night. I probably tripped on some of that wretched broken pathway and bumped my head."

She said nothing.

꙳

THE EVENING WAS enjoyable because of my host's obvious delight in hearing that he was very likely to be the owner of a First Folio within the next few weeks. How it was to be transported to him was a minor problem, though I warned that it would have to be done before Christmas or he would not get the volume until the spring—the monastery is usually snowed in between early January and March. He suggested the best and safest way was for me to travel to collect it—I knew the place, I would be trusted and naturally both the book and I would be heavily insured. But everything in me recoiled at the idea of returning to Saint Mathieu, not because of the responsibility of carrying the book but because I felt that anything might happen in that place, as it already had happened, and I did not trust that I could travel there and back without the return of something that would once again cause me to experience terror. Because I realized that, other than the slight mishap today, I had never actually come to any real harm. What I had experienced was the extremes of fear and they were dreadful enough for me to want to avoid them at all cost. I could not speak of any of this. I simply said that I felt a professional firm used to transporting items of great value would be better bringing the Folio to England. I knew one which was entirely reliable, if costly, and Sir Edgar agreed to let me suggest the arrangement to the monastery once the deal had been finally agreed and the money paid.

IT WAS A CLOSE, thundery end to the day. The doors were open onto the garden and we could see the odd flash of lightning over the sea in the distance. Sir Edgar had brought up a bottle of fine old brandy to celebrate his latest acquisition and we talked on until late. Lady Alice glanced at me occasionally and I sensed that she was concerned, but she said nothing more until we were going upstairs just after midnight.

"Mr. Snow, I have been rummaging about and finding some more things about the White House and its garden, if you are still interested. I have set them out in the small study for you—do look at them tomorrow if you would like to. But perhaps you've had enough of all that after your visit there today. I spoke to a friend who lives not far away and she said the place has been quite derelict and shut up for some years now. Everyone wonders why no one has bought it or had it restored. It seems terrible for it to be allowed to fall to bits like that. Anyway, I wish you a good rest and you know where the small study is if you do want to have a look through what I found."

I had bidden her goodnight and closed my door, walked to the window and was standing looking out into the darkness and listening to the thunder, which was now rolling inland toward the house, before the meaning of what Lady Alice had said hit me.

It was hopeless then to try and sleep. I read for a while but the words slid off the surface of my mind. I opened the window. It was raining slightly and the air was heavy, but there was the chill of autumn on it.

I put on my dressing gown, but as I moved toward the door the bedside lamp went out. There was a small torch lantern beside it for just this eventuality and by the

light of it I made my way quietly across the wide landing and down the passage that led to the small study.
My torch threw its beam onto the wood paneling and
the pictures on the walls beside me, mainly rather heavy
oils of ancient castles and sporting men. Sir Edgar had
a very fine collection of eighteenth-century watercolors
in the house but up here nothing was of much beauty
or interest. Once or twice my torch beam slipped over
the eyes of a man or a dog, once over a set of huge teeth
on a magnificently rearing stallion and the eyes and the
teeth gleamed in the light. The thunder cracked almost
overhead and lightning sizzled down the sky.

I found a number of magazines and newspapers laid
out on the round table, opened at articles about the
White House and its garden, but there were none of the
photographs I had been given a glimpse of earlier, though
I looked closely for the picture of myself, as a small boy,
sitting on the bench with Hugo and the other child, presumably a friend. There was no reason why it would
be here, of course—these were all photographs taken
professionally, showing the splendor of the garden in its
heyday, the royal visit. Two things made me shine the
torch closely and bend over to peer at them. One was a
photograph of Denisa Parsons. I had seen her before in
the magazine Lady Alice had first shown me but here she
was, I guessed, a decade older. She was a smart woman,
her hair pulled back, wearing a flowered afternoon
dress, earrings. Her head was thrown back and she was
beaming as she pointed something out proudly to the
King. I looked closely at her features. There seemed pre-

cious little resemblance between this handsome woman with the rather capacious, silk-covered bosom and the ragged, wispy-haired figure in the ancient mackintosh who had greeted me that afternoon. But faces change over the years, features decay, flesh shrivels, skin wrinkles and discolors, hair thins, teeth fall out. I could not be sure either way.

The second item was a long article from *The Times* about Denisa Parsons, the famous garden creator, internationally celebrated for what she had done at the White House. Pioneer. Plantswoman. Important Designer. Garden Visionary. The praise was effusive.

There was little about either her earlier life or her family, merely a mention of an ordinary background, marriage to Arthur Parsons, a Civil Servant in the Treasury, and two children, Margaret and Michael.

The paper was dated some thirty years ago.

I went back to my room, where the lamp had come on again. The storm was still prowling round and I could see lightning flickering across the sky occasionally as I lay in bed, sleepless.

Do I believe in ghosts? The question is common enough and, if asked, I usually hedge my bets by saying, "Possibly." If asked whether I have seen one, of course until now I have always said that I have not. I had not seen the ghost, for ghost it must surely be, to whom the small hand belonged, but I had felt it often enough, felt it definitely and unquestionably a number of times. I had even grown accustomed to it. Once or twice I realized that I was expecting to feel it holding my own hand.

But in some strange way, the small hand was different, however ghostly it might be. Different? Different from the woman at the White House. Was she a ghost? Or had she been, as I had first assumed, a visitor, or even a squatter in the empty place, an old bag lady pretending to be Denisa Parsons? Someone who had once worked for her perhaps? The more I thought about it, the more likely that explanation seemed. It was sad to think that someone had gone back there, broken in and was living among the dirt and debris, like a rat, bundled into old clothes and spending the time looking through old scrapbooks and albums of the place in its heyday. But people do end their days in such a state, more often, I think, than we know.

It was only as I felt myself relax a little and begin to slip down into sleep that I remembered the part of the garden to which she had led me and which was tended and kept up, the grass mown, the hedges clipped, as if in preparation for opening to a party of visitors. I was confused about the place. I had walked across so many different stretches of lawn, gone through several arches cut in the yards and yards of high dark hedge, down steps, toward other enclosures, so that I had no sense of where the abandoned garden ended and the tended area began. And how many pools were there and where had the bench been on which I had apparently sat with my brother and our friend?

I drifted from remembering it all into dreaming about it, so that the real and the unreal slid together and I was walking in and out of the various parts of the garden, trying to find the right gap in the hedge, wanting to leave but endlessly sent back the way I had come, as happens to one in a maze.

I was alone, though. There was no old woman and even though at one point I seemed to have turned into myself as a boy, there were no other boys with me. Only at one point, as I tried to find my way out through yet another archway, I felt the small hand leading me on, though it felt different somehow, as befitted my dream state, an insubstantial hand which had no weight or density and which I could not grasp as I could the firm and very real flesh and bone of the hand that tucked itself into mine in my real and waking life.

Nineteen

I left for London the following morning feeling un-refreshed—I had slept, fitfully, for only a few hours and felt strung up but at least I left Sir Edgar a happy man and he had given me a new commission. He had become interested in late medieval psalters and wanted to know if I could obtain a fine example of an illuminated one. It was a tall order. Such things came on to the market very rarely, but putting out feelers, talking to people in the auction houses in both London and America, email-ing colleagues, even contacting the Librarian at Saint Mathieu des Etoiles, would be very enjoyable and keep my mind away from the business at the White House. I also had some nineteenth-century salmon fishing diaries to sell for another client.

I even drove some twenty miles further, taking an indi-rect route back in order to avoid going anywhere near the lane leading to that place, though I knew I would not succeed in forgetting it. But I told myself sternly that speculation was fruitless.

As I neared London the traffic was heavy and I was stationary for some fifteen minutes. There was nothing remotely unusual about the place—an uninteresting stretch of suburban road. I was not thinking of the house or the garden or the hand, I was making a mental list of people I could contact with my various client requirements, remembering someone in Rome, and another in Scotland who might well be interested in the fishing books.

I glanced at the stationary traffic in the opposite lane, then in my rear-view mirror at a lorry. It did not matter that I was delayed. I had no appointment to rush to. I was simply bored.

I cannot say that anything happened. It is very difficult to explain what took place, or did not, as I waited in my car. Anyone would tell me that my imagination had been thoroughly wound up and become overexcited and likely to react to the slightest thing, because of the events of the past few weeks, and they would be right. And that is the point. My imagination did not play tricks, I heard, saw, sensed, smelled, felt nothing. Nothing. There was nothing. The strongest sensation was one of nothingness, as if I had been abandoned in some way. Nothing would come near me again, I would not be troubled or contacted. Nothing. I would never feel the sensation of the small hand in mine, or wonder if I was being watched, if something was trying to lure me into whatever lay ahead. Nothing. There was nothing. It had left me, like a fever which can suddenly, inexplicably lift, like the mist that clears within seconds.

Nothing.

I was entirely alone in my car, as the traffic began to nudge slowly forward, and I would be alone when I reached my flat. If I went back to the White House, or to the monastery, I would be alone and there would never again be a child dashing across the road through the storm in the path of my moving car.

Nothing.

I felt an extraordinary sense of release.

Half an hour later, as I walked into my flat, I knew that it had not been a fantasy, or even wishful thinking. I was free and alone, whatever it was had left me and would not return. How does one account for such strong convictions? Where had they come from and how?

Would I miss the small hand? I even wondered that for a fleeting second, because before it had begun to urge me into dangerous places, it had been strangely comforting, as if I had been singled out for a particular gentle gesture of affection from the unseen.

But the one thing I could not forget was the photograph the old woman had shown me of Hugo, his friend and me in the White House garden. I certainly had no recollection of the day or the place, but that was not surprising. I could only have been about five years old— though in the way details remain, I had remembered the Fair Isle jumper so clearly. I would ring Hugo when he was back from the States and ask him about it, though I really had no particular reason for my continuing interest except that coincidence sometimes forms a pleasing symmetry.

✎

A COUPLE OF days later, I had a call from a dealer in New York who had a couple of items I had long been in search of and, as there were various other books I could ask about for clients while I was there, I left on a trip which then took me to San Francisco and North Carolina. I was away for three weeks, returned and flew straight off again to Munich, Berlin and then Rome and back to New York. By the time I was home, several missions having been successfully accomplished, it was late September. I was so involved with work in London for the following week or so that I completely forgot everything that had happened to me and the business of the photograph did not cross my mind.

And then I came in after dining with a potential client from Russia, to find a message from Hugo on my answerphone.

"Hi, Bro . . . it's been ages . . . wondered if you fancied coming up here next weekend. Benedicte's playing a concert in the church—you'd like it. Time we caught up anyway. Give us a call."

I did so and we arranged that I would drive up to Suffolk the following Friday evening. Hugo always had an early start to his school day, so I didn't keep him long on the phone, but as we were about to ring off, I said, "By the way . . . I don't suppose you remember this any more than I do—but when we were kids, did we go with the folks to see a garden in Sussex? It was called the White House."

I do not know what I expected Hugo to say—probably that he had no more idea than I did.

Instead, he said nothing. There was complete silence for so long that I asked if he was still there. When he did reply, his voice sounded odd.

"Yes," he said, "here."

"You don't remember anything about it, do you?"

Another silence. Then, "Why are you asking this?"

"Oh, I just happened upon a photograph of us there—sitting on a bench outside. You, me and a friend."

"No. There was no friend."

"So you do remember it?"

"There was no friend. I'll see you on Friday."

"Yes, but hang on, you . . ."

But Hugo had put the phone down.

Twenty

I arrived in time to change quickly and go along to the church where Benedicte was playing oboe in the concert, both as orchestral member for the Bach and as soloist in the Britten *Metamorphoses*. It was a fine and rather moving occasion and neither Hugo nor I felt inclined to chat as we walked back to the house. It was a chilly night with bright stars and the faint smell of bonfires lingering on the air. Autumn was upon us.

But it was not only our rather contemplative mood after the music that prevented conversation. I could feel the tension coming from Hugo like an unspoken warning, something I had not known since the days of his illness. It was almost tangible and its message was clear—don't talk to me, don't ask questions. Back off. I was puzzled but I knew better than to try and break down the barbed-wire defenses he had put up against me and we reached the house in silence.

The orchestra and performers were being given refreshments elsewhere so we had supper to ourselves, an awkward supper during which I told Hugo half-heartedly about the First Folio and something about my foreign trips, he told me tersely about Katerina's university plans and that he was wondering whether to apply for headships. If he wanted to progress up the schools career ladder, now was the time. I don't think I had ever had such a strained hour with my brother and, as we cleared up the plates, I said that I thought I would go early to bed.

But as I turned, Hugo said, "There's something you ought to know. Have a whisky."

We went into his study. By day this cozy room which overlooks the garden and the path to the river is flooded with light from the East Anglian sky. Now the curtains were closely drawn. Hugo switched the gas fire on, poured us drinks. Sat down. He stared into his glass, swirling the topaz liquid round, and did not speak.

I knew I should wait, not try and hurry him but after several silent minutes I said, "You remember all that stuff I told you . . . panic attacks and so forth?"

Hugo glanced at me and nodded. His expression was wary.

"You were right—they just stopped. Went. It all stopped. Whatever it was."

"Good."

Then I said, "You'd better tell me."

He swirled the whisky again, then drank it quickly.

"The other boy," he said. "I was there, you were there. On the bench. Then you say there was another boy? A friend, you called him. How old was he?"

I tried to bring the photograph to mind. I could see my boy-self, in the Fair Isle jumper. Hugo—I didn't remember Hugo clearly at that age, one never does, but it was Hugo.

"So far as I remember . . . younger than either of us, which made me wonder how he could have been a friend one of us had brought. Short hair, short grey trousers . . . oh, you know, like us. Just a younger boy like us."

"What was his face like?"

I tried again but it was not clear. I had only seen the photograph once, although I had stared at it hard, in my surprise, for some moments.

I shook my head.

"There was no other boy," Hugo said.

I opened my mouth to say that of course there was another boy, he had not seen the photograph and I had, but Hugo's face was pale and very serious.

He got up and poured us both a second whisky and, as he handed me mine, I noticed that his hand was shaking.

"The story," he said at last, "is this. We went twice. To that place."

"The White House? That garden? What do you mean?"

"Mother took us. I was at prep school . . . at Millgate. I was out for the weekend. She brought you. It was an outing."

I remembered little about Hugo being away at school then, though there was always a strange sense of loss, a loneliness, a hollowness at the center of my everyday life, but by the time I was old enough to understand what it meant I had gone away to school myself, and Hugo was at Winchester.

"A boy drowned."

I heard the words in the quiet room but it took me a moment to make sense of them.

"A boy . . ."

"He was the grandson—of the woman. That woman."

"Denisa Parsons?"

"Her grandson. He was small—two? Something like that. Quite small. He drowned in the lily pond. In the garden."

I looked at my brother. His eyes seemed to have sunken back into their sockets and his face was now deathly pale.

"How do you know this? Did someone tell you? Did mother . . ."

"I was there," Hugo said. His voice was low and he seemed to be speaking half to himself. "I was there."

"What do you mean, 'there'? At that place? Do you mean in the garden? Were we all there?"

"No. You and mother had gone to some other part—there were high hedges . . . arches . . . you'd gone through. You were somewhere else."

He took a sip of whisky. "I don't remember very much. I was by myself in the garden where there was—a big pool. With fish. Golden fish. Then there was—the boy. He was there. I don't remember. But he drowned. The rest is—is what we were told. Not what I remember.

I remember nothing." He looked directly across at me and his eyes seemed suddenly brilliant.

"*I remember nothing.*"

I heard Benedicte's car draw up outside and, after a moment, the front door. Hugo did not move.

"One thing," I managed to say after a moment, "one thing doesn't make sense. The child. The little boy fell into the pool and drowned, but what has that to do with the other boy with us in the photograph? The boy on the bench. We were both older. I don't know why she took us back—do you?"

He shrugged. "I remember nothing."

"Not the second visit? But you were older—what, eleven?"

"And how much do you remember of when you were eleven?"

There were footsteps across the hall and then the wireless being turned on low in the kitchen. My brother stood up.

"Hugo."

"No," I said. "You started to say something, you can't leave it. You said there was no boy in the photograph. But I saw a boy. I saw him as clearly as I saw you. As I saw myself."

He hesitated. Then waved a hand dismissively. "Some tale," he said. "Always is some tale. About a boy who comes back to the garden—that boy."

"What do . . . a boy who comes back?"

"Come on. I don't believe in ghosts, nor do you."

"Oh, as to that . . . you know what happened to me.

Hugo . . ." I went and put my hands on his shoulders, almost shaking him in my rising anger—for it was anger, anger with him for knowing something and trying to keep it from me. "Tell me."

He waited until I had let my hands drop. Then he said, "A boy—that boy I suppose. He was said to go back to the garden—ghosts do that, don't they, so the tales go? Return to the place where whatever happened—happened. He was supposed to. That's all. Just a tale."

"But the boy who was drowned was small—two years old. This one in the photograph was older . . . it can't be the same. This boy in the picture was a real boy, not a ghost."

"How do you know? How do you know what a ghost looks like? White and wispy? Half there?" He laughed, an odd little dry laugh. "The ghost went back there every year and every year he was one year older. He was growing up—like a real boy."

"That's not . . ."

"What? Not possible?"

I fell silent. None of the things that happened were possible in any normal, rational person's world. But they had happened.

"How do you know all this? You lied to me."

"Did I?"

"When I first told you about the small hand in mine, about . . ."

"Oh, for God's sake, that? I shouldn't think that's got anything to do with it, should you? That was just you having a bit of a turn. Coincidence. No, no, forget about it. But if you want to know, the whole story is on the Internet. One of those spook haunting sites. I happened to be looking one night—for the boys. We'd been reading *The Turn of the Screw* . . . you know how it is. You start browsing around . . ." He laughed the short laugh again. "Can't remember what it was called but you'll find it there. The White House ghost . . . all good fun."

He drained the last of his whisky, picked up both glasses and went toward the door without saying another word. I sat on for a moment. I heard his voice, then Benedicte's, low brief snatches of talk.

I felt suddenly exhausted and my head had begun to ache. I wanted to piece together what Hugo had told me, join it up with the things that I had witnessed in the garden to make a whole picture, but they were as disconnected as jigsaw bits in my mind. I was too tired. They would come together, though, I didn't doubt it.

I might look up the story on the Internet, but something about the way my brother had talked didn't ring true. I believed he had found the story on a website, but not by accident when looking up Henry James.

᛭

THE NEXT MORNING, Hugo had gone across to school by the time I came down for breakfast, and in the afternoon he was refereeing a football match, which he did for fun, not because he was on the sports teaching team. Benedicte and I went out into the Suffolk countryside looking at churches, and ended up at a bookshop which also served teas. Over a pot, and some excellent scones, I asked her if Hugo had mentioned my brief spell of panic attacks, and whether he ever had a recurrence of them himself.

"No and no," she said, looking surprised. "Adam, poor you. People often laugh at such things, but they are truly awful. No, his breakdown was over and done. But I wonder, now you say this, if there was anything connecting you?"

"Runs in the family, you mean?" I shook my head. "I doubt it. A lot of people have what I had."

"And have you an idea why you had? Is there not always a reason?"

I hesitated, then shrugged.

She smiled. "Well, it is all over now I hope?"

"Oh yes."

"That's good. Because for Hugo too . . . nothing ever came back. He is now very strong and sane."

❧

WE DROVE HOME through the darkening lanes, talking a little about music and books, more about Katerina and her prospects for getting into Cambridge to read medicine, and as we did so I felt a strange sense of lightness and well-being. The ghost story my brother had told me had explained a great deal. That the small child who had accidentally drowned should have returned to the place and wanted to be with other children seemed natural and I knew people had taken "photographs" of ghosts. I had even seen one, a whole-school photograph with a ghostly master on the far end of the back row—though I confess I had always thought it some sort of fake. But those fakes, easy now with digital cameras, were once not so readily accomplished and as far as I could remember the boy had not looked in any way ghostly in the photograph the old woman had shown me. If he had, surely I would not just have accepted him as a third boy—our unknown "friend."

As I drove, I thought of the small hand, which I now believed to belong to the drowned boy. I had ventured into that place and he had caught hold of me. Had he found me every time I went near water and especially near pools? It seemed so. But why did he urge me forward? Why did I feel such fear of what might be about to happen? I shivered. It seemed beyond belief that he had such ghostly will and power that he could urge me to fall into water and drown and so join him. But what other explanation was there?

We turned into the town and drove down past the main school buildings toward the house.

Well, it was over. The ghostly power had faded. The only puzzle that remained was my visit to the White House when I had met the old woman. Had she been a ghost too? No, she had been real and substantial, though odd, but then, surviving alone in that near-derelict place would drive anyone mad. The drowned child had been her grandson and perhaps he haunted her too, perhaps she felt the small hand in hers, perhaps he took her down those gardens which led out of one another, to the place where the pool had been and that was now just a fairy ring in the ground. Poor woman. She needed help and care and company, but the world often throws up slightly deranged people like her, living on in a dream world, clinging to the past among ruins of its places. Presumably she would die there, alone, starving or ill, or in the aftermath of some accident. I wondered if I could return and talk to her again, persuade her to accept help, even to leave that dreadful, melancholy place in which her whole past life was bound up but which was not somewhere a once handsome, successful, celebrated woman should end her days. I determined to do that. And perhaps at the back of my mind was the thought that I would ask her, gently and tactfully, about her grandson, and whether the photograph was indeed of him as he might have been a few years after his death. And if she was visited by the small hand.

Even though it had left now, and I was quite free and quite unafraid, I could not yet forget the feel of it holding mine, or the effect its power had had on me.

❧

AS WE WENT in I started to wonder if I could make the journey down to Sussex again. In any case, I expected to have news for Sir Edgar Merriman about his psalter, though I might have to take another trip to New York first. New York in the fall has a wonderful buzz, the start of the season in the auction houses, lots of new theater, lots of good parties, the restaurants all full, but the weather still good for walking about. I felt a small dart of excitement.

AFTERWARD, I WAS to remember that delightful sense of anticipation at the thought of New York, my last carefree, guilt-free, blithe moment. Aren't there always those moments, just before the blow falls that changes things forever?

I went into the house behind Benedicte, who was saying that it was strange the lights were not on, that Hugo must be having a drink with the footballers, though he did not usually linger after a match. It had been a pleasant autumn day but there was a chill on the air as we had come up the path, as if there might even be a frost that night, and now I sensed that the house itself was unusually cold.

"What is . . ." I heard Benedicte's voice falter, as she went into the sitting room. "Oh no . . . has there been a burglar in here?"

I went quickly into the room. The French windows that led to the garden were wide open. Benedicte was switching on the lamps, but as we looked round it was clear that nothing had been disturbed or, so far as we could see, taken.

"You stay here," I said. "I'll check."

I went round the entire house at a run but every room was as usual, doors closed, orderly, empty.

"Adam?" Her voice sounded odd.

"Nothing and nobody there. It's all OK. Maybe you forgot to close them when we went out."

"I didn't open them. Nobody opened them."

"Hugo?"

"Hugo had gone to school."

"Well, maybe he came back. Forgot his kit or—something."

"He took his kit and why would he open these doors even if he had not?"

"He'll tell us when he gets back. I can't think of any other explanation, can you?"

There was something in her face, some look of dread or anxiety. I led her into the kitchen and opened a bottle of red wine, poured us both a large glass.

"What can I do to help with supper? Potatoes to peel, something to get from the freezer?"

Benedicte was always well organized, she would have everything planned out, even if the time we would eat was uncertain.

"Yes," she said. I could see from her face that she was anxious. "Some potatoes to wash and put in the oven. Baked potatoes. Sausage casserole. I thought . . ."

I went over to her and put my hand on her shoulder. "You haven't been burgled," I said. "No one has been in here. Don't worry. Hugo will be back any minute. He can look round as well if you like. But nobody's here."

"No," she said.

We made preparations for supper and then took our drinks into the sitting room. I had closed and bolted the windows and drawn the heavy curtains. Benedicte switched on the gas fire. We talked a little. I read some of the paper, she went back to check the oven. Everything was as usual.

The phone rang.

❦

"ADAM?"

She did not look worried then. Only puzzled.

"That was someone from school. They wanted Hugo."

"Yes?"

"Gordon Newitt."

I did not understand.

"The Head of Sports. He wanted Hugo. I said he was probably still having a drink with the team. But he said Hugo wasn't refereeing anything this afternoon. There was only one match and that was away. He wasn't there."

She came further into the room and sat down suddenly. "He wasn't refereeing any match." She said it again in a dull voice, but her expression was still one of bewilderment, as if she were trying to make sense of what she had heard.

It may sound unbelievable to say that it was then that I knew, at that precise moment. That I knew everything, as if it had been given to me whole and entire and in every detail. I knew.

But then what I knew shattered into fragments again

and I heard myself saying that the sports master had surely got it wrong, that perhaps Hugo had swapped places with someone without saying so, or that he might have gone elsewhere and confused his diary, hadn't had time to tell us, that . . .

I heard my own voice babbling uselessly on, saw Benedicte watching my face, as if she would read there what had really happened, where Hugo was.

And then there was a long and terrible moment of silence before I got up.

"I think I should ring the police," I said.

Twenty-one

There is not much more of the story to tell. Hugo's body was found at first light the following morning, some way downriver. He had no injuries and the post-mortem revealed only that he had died by drowning, but not that there had been any natural reason why he should have fallen into the water—after a sudden stroke or heart attack while walking close to the edge. There was no note in the house left for his wife, no hint of any reason why he had lied about being out at the football match. We learned that he had been in school teaching on the Saturday morning, as usual and as he had said he would be. Around twelve-forty, several people had spotted him walking down the high street in the direction of home. After that, no one had seen him at all.

The towpath at that time of year is quiet but there is still the occasional dog-walker or runner. Not that afternoon.

Had he simply tripped or slipped, Benedicte asked again and again. The towpath was dry—they had had no rain for weeks, but he could have stumbled on a tree root.

It was a dreadful time. I stayed until Katerina arrived home from Cambridge and on the Monday morning I had to take Benedicte to identify Hugo's body formally.

We drove to the hospital in silence. She had been very brave and resolute, determined not to break down, and she was determined now, but she said she was afraid that she would collapse when she had to see him. That was why she wanted me with her.

I was as shocked as she was, but I had twice before had to identify bodies of the dead, including that of our father, so I did not feel any sort of fear that morning, merely a great sadness.

It was only when I looked at the still, cold body of my brother lying there that a great wave of realization and horror broke over me. The expression on his face was blank, as it always becomes eventually, no matter what it may have been at the moment of death. It is the blank of eternal sleep.

And then I glanced at his hands. The left one was resting normally, in a relaxed position on the covering sheet. But the right one was not relaxed. Hugo's right hand was folded over, almost clenched. It looked as if it had been holding something tightly.

Of course I knew and then I understood it all, understood that the small hand which had relinquished mine for the last time had not given up, the boy had not gone away but, having failed with me, had moved to Hugo and begun to take his hand, and so draw him, clutching hard, toward the nearest water. I had not given in. I had saved myself, or been saved, though how I did not know then and I still do not know. I had not yielded to the small hand. My brother had, and died, like the boy, by drowning.

I TOLD BENEDICTE none of this. We left the hospital in silence and by late that afternoon Katerina had arrived home. I left them together, partly because I felt that was what they wanted and needed but would never say, partly because I was desperate to get away. I would return for the funeral, of course, but that was not for ten days.

I drove fast away from the town and the river, desperate to put it far behind me.

I felt guilty that I had survived. I was appalled by what I knew had happened to Hugo, even though in the absence of any evidence to the contrary the coroner would record a verdict of accidental death. I would have to live with what I knew and I wondered if many others had been haunted in the same way, those who had once visited the White House garden and felt the touch of the small hand. I surely had not been the first, but I prayed that Hugo had been the last and that now the ghost of the wretched drowned boy could rest in peace.

Twenty-two

I thought that was an end to it. I thought there would be no more to tell. But there is more, another small piece of knowledge I was given and which I can never give back, can never un-know. Another, far worse thing which I must live with, for there is nothing, nothing at all, I can do with it.

When I got back home, I found a letter. It had been posted on the Saturday morning and it was addressed in my brother's hand and for a split second as I looked at the writing I forgot that he was dead but was fleetingly puzzled that he should be writing to me, on paper with pen and ink, not telephoning or sending a quick email.

But then, of course, I remembered. I realized. My hand shook as I opened the envelope, sitting at my desk beside the window on that late afternoon of a gathering sky.

Adam,

You need to know this. I have never been able to tell you, though there have been times in these past days and weeks when I have been close to it. But in the end, I could not. Perhaps you knew I had something to say to you. Perhaps not.

Now, having decided I can live with it no longer, I must tell you.

Please remember that we were children. I was a child. At eleven years old one is still a child. I tell myself so.

The boy drowned because I pushed him into that pool. No one else was there for a moment. No one saw what happened. You came to find me and I grabbed your hand and pulled you away, up the steps and through the archway in that high hedge that has loomed so darkly through my nightmares ever since.

No one knew. It was late in the afternoon, people were leaving the gardens. We were last. I pulled you across the grass until we found Mother and then we left too.

Nothing happened for some years. I pushed it down into my unconscious, as people do with such terrible secrets. Nothing happened until my breakdown, which began suddenly and perhaps half by chance, after I read some story in the paper about a child who had drowned in a similar pool.

I had the same urges you suffered, to throw myself into water. The only difference seems to have been that I did not have to endure the grip of the small hand as you did. Not until it abandoned you—perhaps I should say "gave up on you"—and came to me, not many weeks ago. I knew then that I should be unable to resist it, that I would have to do what it wanted, go with it. Of course I have to. It was my fault. I am guilty. You did nothing. You knew nothing.

I am sorry for this, for what I am telling you, for leaving everyone, for putting my family through what I know will be great pain. One thing, please. I beg you never to tell Benedicte or Katerina, however much you may want to unburden yourself. They will have enough to carry. Please keep this last secret between the two of us.

You are reading this in the knowledge that I have paid my debt and please God that is enough. That is an end to it all. The small ghost and I are at peace. The last hand that other small hand will take hold of will be mine.

With my love
Hugo

Dolly

Iyot Lock

An autumn night and the fens stretch for miles, open and still. It is dark, until the full moon slides from behind a cloud and over the huddle of grey stone which is Iyot Lock. The hamlet straddles a cross roads between flat field and flat field, with its squat church on the east side, hard by Iyot House and the graveyard in between. On the west side, a straggle of cottages leads to Iyot Farm, whose flat fields bleed into the flat fens with no apparent boundary.

❧

IT IS RARE for a night here to be so still. The wind from the sea keens and whistles, though that sea is some miles away. Birds cry their eerie cries.

And then, a slight, thin movement of the air, from inland. It skims over the low dikes and watery ditches, rattles the dry reeds and rushes, rustles the grasses along the roadside.

It strengthens to a low wind and the wind weaves through the few trees in the churchyard and taps the branches of the creeper against the windows of Iyot House.

Nobody hears, for the house is empty and surely the sleepers in the churchyard are not disturbed.

The grasses whisper, the wind moves among the gravestones. And somewhere just about here, by the low wall, another sound, not like the grass but like paper rustling. But there is no paper.

The creeper scrapes the windowpanes. The moon slips out, silvering the glass.

The wind prowls around Iyot Lock, shifting the branches, stirring the grasses, swaying faintly, and from somewhere nearby, hidden or even buried, the sound of rustling.

PART ONE

One

It was a November afternoon when I returned to Iyot Lock and saw that nothing had changed. It was as I recalled it from forty years earlier, the sky as vast, the fen as flat, the river as dark and secretly flowing as it had been in my mind and memory. There had sometimes been sunshine, the river had gleamed and glinted, the larks had soared and sung on a June day, but this was how I knew it best, this landscape of dun and steel, with the sky falling in on my head and the wind keening and the ghosts and will-o'-the-wisps haunting my childhood nights.

I DROVE OVER Hoggett's bridge, seeing the water flow sluggishly beneath, and across the flat straight road, past the old lock keeper's cottage, abandoned now, but then the home of the lock keeper with a wen on his nose and one glass eye, who looked after his sluices and his eel traps in sullen silence. I used to steer clear of Mr. Norry, of whom I was mortally, superstitiously afraid. But the blackened wood and brick cottage was empty and the roof fallen in. As I went by, a great bird with ragged wings rose out of it and flapped away, low over the water.

❧

I COULD SEE far ahead to where the fen met the sky and the tower of Iyot Church, and then the house itself shimmered into view, hazy at first in the veils of rain, then larger, clearer, darker. The only trees for miles were the trees around the churchyard and those close to Iyot House, shading it from sight of the road, though few people, now as ever, were likely to pass by.

❧

I PARKED BESIDE the church wall and got out. The rain was a fine drizzle lying like cobwebs on my hair and the shoulders of my coat. Mine was the only car, so unless she had parked at the house, I was the first to arrive. That did not surprise me.

I pushed open the heavy greened wood of the gate and walked up the path to the church door. Crumpled chicken wire had been used to cover the arch and keep out birds, but it had loosened and old twigs and bits of blackened straw poked through where they had still managed to nest. I lifted the iron handle, twisted it and the door creaked open. The cold inside the porch made me catch my breath. Beyond the inner door, inside the church itself, it was more intense still and smelled of damp stone and mold. It seemed to be the cold of centuries and to seep into my bones as I stood there.

I did not remember anything about the church, though I was sure I must have been there on Sundays, with my aunt—I had a folk memory of the hard polished pews against my bony little backside and legs, for I had been a thin child. It was dull and pale, with uninteresting memorial tablets and clear glass windows that let the silvery daylight in onto the grey floor. Even the Lion and Unicorn, the only touch of color in the church, painted in red and faded gold and blue on a wooden panel, and which might have taken the attention of a small boy, was quite unfamiliar. Perhaps my memories had been of another church altogether.

I wandered about, half expecting to hear the door open and see her standing there, but no one came and my footsteps were solitary on the stone floor.

The lights did not come on when I clicked the switch and the church was dim in the sullen November afternoon. I made my way out again, but as I stood looking out at the path and the graveyard, I had a strange and quite urgent sense that I ought to do something, that I was needed, that I was the one person who could rescue—rescue what? Who? I could not remember when I had had such an anxious feeling and as I walked out, it became stronger, almost as if someone were tugging at my sleeve and begging me to help them. But there was no one. The churchyard was empty and it felt desolate in the gathering dusk, with the brooding sky overhead, though it was only just after three o'clock.

I shook myself, to be rid of the inexplicable feeling and walked briskly to the car and drove the short distance to the house, the back and chimneys of which were hard to the road. There were the wooden gates, which I remembered well. If I opened them I could swing into the yard and park behind the scullery and outhouses, but the gate was locked and seemingly barred on the inside, so I returned to the lay-by beside the church and set out to walk back along the deserted lane to Iyot House. I glanced down the road but there was no sight of a car, even far away, no moving dot in the distance.

And then, it was as if something were tugging at my sleeve, though I felt nothing. I was being urged to return to the churchyard and I could not disobey, whatever was asking me to go there needed something—needed me? What did it want me to do and why? Where exactly was I to go?

I turned again, feeling considerably annoyed but unable to resist, and the moment I set off I sensed that this was right, and that who or whatever wanted me there was relieved and pleased with me. We all like to please by doing the thing we are being asked, in spite of our misgivings, and so I retraced my steps briskly the hundred yards to the lych gate. That was not quite far enough. I must go through and into the churchyard. By now the dark was gathering fast and I could barely see my way, but there were still streaks of light in the sky to the west and it was not a large area. I moved slowly among the gravestones.

It was almost as if I were playing the old childhood game of Hide and Seek, one in which the inner sense was saying "Cold" "Cold" "Warm" "Very Warm."

It was as I neared three gravestones that were set against the low wall at the back that the sense of urgency became very strong. I went to each one. All were ancient, moss and lichen-covered and the names and dates were no longer visible. Even as I got near to the first I felt a peculiar electric shock of heat, followed immediately by a sense of release. This was it. I was there. But where? Wherever I was meant to be? Then by whom, and why?

I stood still. The wind was keening, the darkness shrinking in to swallow me. I was not exactly afraid but I was uneasy and bewildered. And then I heard it. It seemed to be coming from the ground in front of a gravestone. I squatted down and listened. The moan of the wind was blocked out by the wall there, and it was very still. At first I could not make it out but after a few moments, I thought it sounded as if something was rustling, a dry sound, like that made by the wind in the reed beds, but softer and fainter. It came from under the grass, under the earth. A rustling, as if someone were . . .

No, I could not tell. I stayed for some minutes and the rustling came again and again, and each time it made me feel as one feels when a name one has forgotten is almost, almost on the tip of the tongue. I knew the sound, I knew what was making it, I knew why . . . but it hovered just out of reach, like the elusive name. I knew and then did not know, I remembered—but then it was gone. I waited for a few more minutes. Nothing else happened, I heard nothing else and not least because by this time I was thoroughly chilled. The east wind was whistling across the fen even more strongly and I left the churchyard and returned to Iyot House.

IT WAS IN pitch darkness and the wind had got up even more in that short time and was dashing the trees against the walls and rattling the ivy. Stupidly I had not brought a torch and had to edge my way through the gate and up the narrow path between thickly overgrown shrubs to the front door. I had the key ready and to my surprise the lock was smooth and opened at a turn. I felt about for a switch—there was none in the porch but once inside the hall I found the panel of them to my left. The hall, staircase and narrow passageway were lit, though the bulbs were quite dim. But at once, the past came rushing toward me as I not only saw but smelled the inside of the house where I had once been a small boy on occasional and always strange visits. The pictures on the wall, one of a half-draped woman by a rock pool, another of sheep in the snow, and two portraits whose eyes pierced me and then seemed to follow me, as they always had, reminded me of the past, the feel of the polished floor beneath the rug at my feet, the great brass dinner gong, the once-polished and gleaming banister, now filmed and dull, reminded me, and the silent grandfather clock, the frieze of brown carnations running along the wallpaper, the dark velveteen curtain hanging on a rod across the drawing room door, all these things reminded me . . . As I looked round I was eight years old again and in Iyot House for the first time, anxious, wary, full of half-fears, jumping at my own shadow as it glided beside me up the stairs.

❧

BUT I WAS not afraid of anything there that late afternoon, merely affected by the atmosphere of sadness and emptiness. Iyot House had never been full of light and fun but it was not a gloomy house either and people who had lived there had looked after me as best they knew, and even loved me—though perhaps I had little sense of it as a boy. I had been afraid of shadows and darkness, of sudden sounds, of spiders and bats but I had never believed Iyot House had any ghosts or malign forces hanging about within its walls, at least not until . . .

I stopped with one foot on the stairs . . . until what? It was teasing me again, that sense of something just out of reach, almost remembered but then fluttering off just as I grasped it.

Until something had happened? Or was it to do with some*one*?

It was no good. I could not remember, it had danced away, to tantalize me yet again.

❧

I WENT AROUND the house, putting on the lights as I did so, and each room came alive at the touch of the switch, bedrooms, dressing rooms, bathrooms, their furniture and curtains and carpets exactly as I had known them, faded now and dusty, with the smell of all rooms into which fresh air had not come through an opened window, for years. I did not feel anything much, not sadness or fondness, just a certain muted nostalgia.

And then I climbed the last steep, short flight of stairs to the attics and at once I felt an odd fluttering sensation in my chest, as though I were reaching somewhere important, where I might at last be able to recall the incident that was nudging at my memory.

This was familiar. This had been my territory. These small rooms with their tiny, iron-latched windows, the narrow single bed, the bare floorboards, had been where I slept, dreamed, thought, played . . . and where I had first encountered Leonora.

I made my way to the room that had been mine. It was the same, and yet quite different, because though the furniture was as I recalled, there were, of course, none of my clothes, toys, games or books, nothing that had made it personal to me, brought it alive. It also seemed far smaller than I had remembered—but, of course, I am a man of six feet two and I was a small boy when I had been here last. I sat on the bed. The mattress was the same, soft but with the springs beneath poking through here and there. I felt them again, digging into my thinly fleshed young back. The wicker chair was almost too small for me to sit in, the window seat narrow and hard. I remembered the wallpaper with its frieze of beige roses, the iron fireplace with the scrolled canopy, the tall cupboard set deep into the wall.

The cupboard. It was something about the cupboard; something in it or that had happened beside it?

I did not want to open it, and though I felt foolish, my hand hovered on the latch for several seconds, and my heart started to beat fast. I did not remember anything except that my mounting distress meant the game was over, I was "hot."

I did open it, of course. It was empty, the shelves dusty. It went some way back and as I took a couple of deep breaths and felt calmer, I reached up and ran my hand along the shelves. Nothing. There was nothing there at all, nothing until I reached the top shelf, so far from me when I was a boy that I had to stand on the stool to reach it, but now easily accessible. Still nothing.

I shook myself, and was about to close the cupboard door when I heard it—a very soft rustling, as if someone were stirring their hand about in crisp tissue paper, perhaps as they unpacked a parcel. It stopped. I opened the door wide again. The rustling was a little louder. I got the old stool, stood on it and felt the top shelf of the cupboard to the very back, where my hand touched the wall. Nothing. It was totally and completely empty.

Nevertheless, there was the sound again, and although it was no louder, it seemed more urgent and agitated.

I lost my nerve, closed the cupboard and fled, running down the stairs to the hall. When I stopped and got my breath back, I listened. The wind was whistling down the chimney and lifting the rug on the floor, but I could no longer hear even the faintest sound of paper rustling.

I WENT INTO the sitting room, thinking to wait for her there but it had such a damp and chill, and the fireplace was full of rubble, so I retreated, switched out the lights and locked the front door. The wind seemed to pare the skin off my face as I turned into the lane and I hastened to get into the car. I would drive back to the market town and my small, warm, comfortable hotel. It was obvious that she was not going to come to Iyot House—perhaps she had never intended it.

But I knew that even if she did come, she would not remember anything. We blot out bad things from our minds and especially when they have been bad things we ourselves have done, in childhood perhaps most of all.

A CHILL MIST was smothering the fen and veils of it writhed in front of the headlights as I drove away. I would be glad to get to the Lion at Cold Eeyle, and a good malt whisky by the fire, even more glad to have the whole thing done with at the solicitor's the next morning. Would Leonora turn up there? I had no doubt that she would. The prospect of inheriting something was just what would bring her up here, as nothing else had ever done—I knew she had not visited Aunt Kestrel in forty years, but then she had lived abroad for the most part, following her mother's example in marrying several times. I did not know if she had any children but I doubted it.

THE LION WAS snug and welcoming, after an unpleasant ten-mile drive through the swirling fog. My room was at the top of the house, down some winding corridors. I spruced up and returned to the bar, a whisky and the log fire.

I ate a good dinner and went to bed early. The place was quiet and when I had got my key, the receptionist said that I was the only person staying. The meeting at the solicitor's was at ten, in his Cold Eeyle office.

I thought about Aunt Kestrel that night, after I had read a dozen pages and put out the light. I had barely known her, wished I had talked to her more about the family and the past she could have told me so much about. She had housed a stiff, shy small boy and a wayward girl when she had no knowledge of children, what they wanted or needed. She could have refused but she had not, feeling strongly, as her generation did, about family ties and family duty. Of course, it had never occurred to me as a boy that she was probably lonely, widowed young, childless, and living in that bleak and isolated house with only the moaning wind, the fogs and rain for company, other than sour Mrs. Mullen.

I fell asleep thinking about the two of them, and about Leonora and how anxious I had been about the way she behaved, when we were children, how she had seemed so careless about bringing wrath down on her own head and curses on the house in general.

I woke and put on the bedside lamp. It was deathly quiet. Obviously the fog had not lifted but was swaddling the land, deadening every sound. Not that there would be many. Cars did not drive around Cold Eeyle at night, people did not walk the streets.

I was about to pick up my book and read a few more pages to lull myself off again, when my ears picked up a slight and distant sound. I knew what it was at once, and it acted like a pick stabbing through the ice of memory. It was the sound of crying. I got up and opened the window. The taste of the fog came into my mouth and its damp web touched my skin. But through its felted layers, from far away, I heard it again, half in my own head, half out there, and then everything came vividly back, the scene with Leonora in Aunt Kestrel's sitting room, her rage, the crack of the china head against the fireplace, my own fear, prompting my heart to leap in my chest. All, all of it I remembered—no, I re-lived, my heart pounding again, as I stood at the window and through the fog-blanketed darkness heard the sound again.

Deep under the earth, inside its cardboard coffin, shrouded in the layers of white paper, the china doll with the jagged open crevasse in its skull was crying.

PART TWO

Two

Two children were traveling, separately from different directions, to Iyot House, Iyot Lock, one hot afternoon in late June.

"Where am I to put them?" Mrs. Mullen had asked, to whom children were anathema. "Where will they sleep?"

Kestrel, the aunt, knew better than to make any suggestion, the housekeeper being certain to object and overrule.

"I wonder where seems best to you?" Images of the bedrooms flicked in a slide show through Aunt Kestrel's mind, each one seeming less suitable than the last—too dark, too large, too full of precious small objects. She had no experience of young children, though she was perfectly well disposed to the thought of having her great nephew and niece to stay, and had a vague idea that they were easily frightened of the dark or broke things. And were they to sleep in adjacent rooms or with a communicating door? On separate floors?

"The attics would suit best, in my view," Mrs. Mullen said.

Shadowy images chased across Kestrel's mind, troubling her enough to make her get up from her writing desk. "I think we had better look. I can't remember when I was last up there."

She went through the house, three flights of wide stairs, one of steep and narrow. Mrs. Mullen did not trouble to follow, knowing it would all be decided satisfactorily.

⌇

THE SUMMER WIND beat at the small latched windows but daylight changed its nature, making it seem a soft wind, and benign. The floorboards were dusty. Kestrel opened a cupboard set deep into the wall. The shelves were lined with newspaper and smelled of nothing worse than mothballs and old fluff. One of the rooms was completely empty, the second contained only a cracked leather trunk, but the two rooms next to one another, in the middle of the row, had furniture—an iron bed in each, a chest of drawers, a mirror. One had a wicker chair, one a musty velvet stool. And cupboards, more cupboards. She had lived here for over forty years and remembered a time when the attic rooms had been for maids. Now, there was Mrs. Mullen, who had the basement, and a woman who came on a bicycle from a village on the other side of the fen.

The rooms could be made right, she thought, though vague as to exactly what children might need to make them so. Curtains? Rugs? Toys?

Well, linen at least.

"The attics," she said, coming down from them, "will do nicely."

~

KESTREL DICKINSON HAD been an only child for fourteen years before two sisters were born, Dora first and then Violet. Dora was plain and brown-eyed with brown straight hair and placid under the spotlight of everyone's attention. Their mother tried to conceal her disappointment, firstly that Dora was not a boy and secondly that she was not beautiful, though her love for both girls was never in doubt. Violet was born two years and two days after Dora and grew into a pert and extremely pretty child, with blonde bubble curls and intensely blue eyes, and was adored. She smiled, lisped, talked early, looked beautiful in frills, never got her clothes dirty, and laughed with delight at everyone who looked in her direction.

From the first Dora hated her and Violet learned quickly to meet like with like. As they grew into children and then young women, they quarreled and despised one another. From the beginning the root of it all was Dora's jealousy, but Violet, who had had her head turned early, quickly turned proud, self-absorbed and boastful. In her turn, Dora behaved with pettiness and spite. Their feud became life-long. Violet married when she was eighteen, and again, at twenty-five and thirty-three. After that she had a succession of lovers but did not bother to marry them. When she was forty-two, she had her first and only child, Leonora, by a rich man called Philip van Vorst, before she embarked on eight years of restless travel, from Kenya to Paris, Peking to Los Angeles, Las Vegas to Hong Kong. Her daughter traveled with her, growing quickly used both to their nomadic life, a succession of substitute fathers, hotels, money and, like her mother, being pretty, spoiled, admired and both lonely and dissatisfied.

Violet rarely returned home, but whenever she did, she and Dora picked up their animosity where it had been left, always finding fresh things about which to quarrel. Violet's frivolous, amoral, butterfly nature infuriated her sister. She knew she behaved better, led a more wholesome life, but never managed to feel that these counted for anything when her sister arrived home showering presents out of her suitcases. The adoration she had always received shone out again from parents, servants, friends, everything that had been complained of was set aside. Dora, plain and brown, simmered in corners and, long into adult life, plotted obscure revenge. Violet had had three husbands, innumerable lovers—usually handsome, always rich—and a daughter with enviable looks. Dora had had one rather anonymous suitor who had never confessed any feelings for her and who had eventually faded from her life over a period of several months, while she remained waiting in hope.

By this time, Kestrel was long married and living at

Iyot House, though she did not have children of her own and had detached herself from her feuding sisters, but had never stopped feeling guilt that she had not somehow succeeded in uniting them.

And then, in the flurry of less than three months, Dora had met and married George Cayley, a local widower almost thirty years her senior. A year later she had produced her small, frail son, Edward. Two years later both she and George were dead.

~

KESTREL INHERITED IYOT House from her own husband after a short marriage. At first she had disliked it and the expanse of dun-colored fens, their watery aspect and huge oppressive skies, the isolation and lack of friends, the oddness of the villagers. In time, though, she grew used to it and found some sort of spirit half-hidden there. She had people to stay in the spring and summer and for the rest of the year was happy with her own company and her painstaking work as a botanical illustrator.

From Violet there came the occasional, erratic postcard which rarely mentioned her daughter Leonora but she heard nothing of her orphaned nephew until a letter had come asking if he might spend the summer at Iyot House. In some desperation she wrote to Violet.

"They are cousins after all and he will need a companion."

It was settled.

Three

"Edward Cayley," he wrote in the steamed-up train window. "Edward Laurence Cayley." Then rubbed it out with his sleeve.

He had been driven from the house by his half-brother's business chauffeur and hurried across the concourse of Liverpool Street as if he must be bundled out of sight as quickly as possible. The driver carried his case; he carried a small hold-all. The station smelled of smoke, which tasted on his tongue and caught the back of his throat. His hold-all and suitcase had labels tied on with his name and the station to which he was traveling. He was put in charge of the guard, inspected, turned round, and then put into the van.

"Two hours." The guard had several missing teeth and the rest were brown.

After that, there was nothing. No one looked at or spoke to him, he had nothing to eat or drink. The train steamed on. He saw cows and churches, fields and houses, dykes and people on bicycles. He did not think and he did not feel, he simply accepted, having learned that accepting was the best and safest way.

He was neither happy nor unhappy: he was a frozen child, as he had been since he had arrived at the house of a half-brother who neither loved nor wanted him but who, with his wife, had looked after him dutifully, without fault or favor.

He was a pale, fair, thin boy, small for his age but fit and wiry now and with a sensitive and intelligent face. He was liked. It was taken for granted that he would find his way easily in life, that excuses would never need to be made for him.

But, looking out at the cows and sheep and churches and dikes and people on bicycles, he was unaware of any of this. He wrapped himself in a bubble of unknowing.

LEONORA VAN VORST travelled alone from Geneva the same day, with her name on a badge pinned to her coat and a brown suitcase covered in shipping line labels, thrown from porter to porter and, finally, to the driver of a hire car which was to take her from Dover to Iyot Lock. To anyone watching her follow the last porter with her case on his shoulder and her round overnight bag in his left hand, across the dock from the boat, she looked small, solemn and lost, but within herself, she was tall, confident and superior. She had money inside her glove for the last tip. The driver loaded her cases and pinched her cheek, feeling sorry for what he thought of as "the little mite." Leonora frowned and climbed into the back of the car without speaking. She was self-possessed, calm, haughty, and without any sense that there was such a thing as love, or vulnerability.

The car sped east and after only a few miles she began to feel sick, but fearing to mention it, and seem weak, she closed her eyes and imagined a sheet of smooth black paper, as her mother had once taught her, and eventually the nausea faded and she slept. Through the rear mirror the driver saw a white-faced child with a halo of red hair spread behind her on the back of the seat, lips pinched together and an expression he could not exactly make out, partly of detachment, partly of something like defiance.

Four

"How do you do?" The boy put out his hand, Aunt . . ."
But his voice wavered on the "Kestrel."

"Lord, I'm not your aunt. You'd better come in."
Mrs. Mullen looked down at the boy's bags, both small.
The taxi had already turned and started down the long
straight road twelve miles back to the station.

"Well, pick them up." She had no intention of waiting on two children.

"Oh. Yes."

She did not know how a boy of eight should look but
Edward Cayley seemed thin, his knee-caps protruding
awkwardly from bony little legs. His hair was freshly
cut, too short, leaving a fringe of bristle on his neck.

"Put them down there."

"Yes."

They stood in the dimness of the hall staring at one
another in silence for a full minute, Mrs. Mullen struck
by an unfamiliar sympathy for a child who was not like

the few children she had known, who had been sturdy, loud, greedy, grubby and disrespectful. That was how village children were. Edward Cayley was the opposite of all those things and though she did not yet know about his appetite, no boy so thin, and pale as a peeled willow, could surely be a big eater.

Edward looked at Mrs. Mullen, and then at his own feet, knowing that staring round a strange house was impolite. He could think of nothing to say, though he wondered who the woman was and where his Aunt Kestrel was, while knowing that the behavior of adults was generally inexplicable.

The house smelled strange, half of living, breathing smells, half of age and damp.

"Wait there."

"Yes."

The woman disappeared into the dimness and a door bumped softly shut. He waited. All he knew was that Aunt Kestrel was related to the dead mother he did not remember and that he was to stay with her at Iyot for some weeks of this summer. He supposed that was enough.

IN HER DRESSING room, Kestrel adjusted her necklace, wondered if she should change it for another, put up her hands to the clasp and froze. The boy was here, and she was anxious. She had seen him once, as a baby of a month old, she did not know what he would be like and she was unused to children, but she was not innately hostile to them like Mrs. Mullen. She wanted to make the boy comfortable, for him to talk to her, find entertainment, not be homesick or bored and now that he was here, her nerve failed her. But at least he would not be lonely.

The house was silent. Mrs. Mullen had announced Edward's arrival and then disappeared. Aunt Kestrel, as she must now think of herself, replaced the necklace and went downstairs.

THEY HAD LUNCH in the dining room, he and the aunt, and he sat quiet, pale and watchful, eating everything he was offered quite slowly, made nervous by the room itself, with its heavy red curtains held back by brass rods, and large portraits of men with horses and dogs and women with hats and distant children.

"Are you enjoying your lunch? Is there anything else you would like?" He sensed with surprise that his aunt was as nervous as he was, and far more anxious to please. His own wish was more negative—not to annoy anyone, not to provoke irritation, not to be chastised, not to break anything. He had been warned so many times about the breaking of objects, of china and ornaments and even windows, that he was in a state of suspended terror, passing by the dresser with its huge dishes, small tables with glass paperweights and gilded figurines.

"Is your drink too strong?"

"It's very nice, thank you."

It was lemon squash diluted so much that the water was barely tinted.

"Do you like lamb chop?"

"Yes, thank you."

"And how was your train journey? Were you properly looked after?"

"Yes, thank you. I traveled in the guard's van with the guard."

"Quite right. But was that uncomfortable?"

It had been. He had been forced to sit on someone's leather trunk, next to cardboard boxes of live chicks which chirped and rustled about and then went still, until they were put out onto a station platform somewhere. But the guard had shared a chocolate bar with him and told him stories about famous railway murders and ghosts in tunnels.

"It was very nice, thank you."

He looked up from his plate at Aunt Kestrel just as she looked straight at him. They took one another in. She looked old to him, with a tweedy skirt and a buttoned blouse, and several rings on her left hand, but her face was soft and not at all unkind.

To her, the boy was alarmingly like his mother in profile, with the same long straight nose and small mouth, but his full face was like no one she recognized. He was nervous, polite and private, his true thoughts and feelings all his own and kept hidden. His manner deterred any questions other than those about the food and drink and his journey.

"Your cousin Leonora will come tomorrow. Have you met her before?"

He shook his head, his mouth full of pears and custard.

"I thought not. She is your Aunt Violet's only child—Violet and your mother were sisters and . . . well, and I was sister to them both, of course. But older. Much older."

He said nothing.

"So you are quite close in age. I hope you'll get on."

He did not know what to say, having no sense at all of what it might be like to spend a whole summer with a girl cousin he had never seen.

"What would you like to do now? Do you have a rest after lunch? I'm afraid I'm not used to—to what children . . . boys . . . do. Have you brought any books to read or do you play with . . . Or you could go into the garden."

He followed her into the hall. "But I expect you'd like to see your room and so on now."

"Thank you."

Mrs. Mullen appeared from behind a baize-covered door.

"I'll take him up then shall I?"

He did not want her to but could not have said and they all three stood about uncertainly for a moment.

"Well, perhaps I should . . . you carry on with the dining room, Mrs. Mullen."

He noted the name.

"Pick those up then," Mrs. Mullen said, pointing to his bags, the small one and the very small.

"Yes."

Edward picked them up and followed his aunt to the stairs.

Five

"At what time should you go up?"

Edward looked up from the solitaire board. Aunt Kestrel had unlocked a cupboard in the drawing room, whose blinds were pulled down all day as well as at night, and found the solitaire, a shove ha'penny board and a pile of jigsaw puzzles which he had taken up to the attics. He examined the glass marbles again. They were wonderful colors, deep sea green, brilliant blue, blood red, and clear glass enclosing swirls of misty grey. The board was carved out of rosewood with green velvet covering the underside.

"Do you have something to eat first, or . . ."

"I have milk and two biscuits at seven and then I go to bed."

"Of course, these are the holidays; I daresay rules should be stretched. When would you like to go up?"

The idea that he could choose his own time, that routine was not made of iron but could be broken, was not only new but alarming.

"I am quite tired," he said, moving a blue marble over a clear glass one, to leave only seven on the board. His aunt had shown him how to play and as it had been raining, he had done so, sitting beside the window, for most of the afternoon. Seven was the smallest number he had got down to without being unable to move again.

"You have had a rather dull day."

"It has been very nice, thank you."

Kestrel was taken aback again by the opaque politeness of the child.

"You will have more fun when Leonora arrives. And this miserable rain. We don't get a lot of rain at Iyot but we do get wind. Wind and skies."

He thought everyone had sky, or skies, but perhaps this was not the case. He didn't ask.

"Five!" he said under his breath, removing another blue.

"Excellent."

Mrs. Mullen brought in a small glass of milk and two garibaldi biscuits on a lacquer tray.

"Thank you very much," he said, stopping in the doorway. "I have had a very nice day."

His earnest, unformed face stayed with Kestrel for a long time after he had gone. He was her own flesh and blood, he was part of her. She did not know him, as she had not known Dora after she had grown up and married, and yet she felt connected to him and his words touched her deeply, his vulnerability impressed itself on her so that she felt suddenly afraid on his behalf and had an urge to protect him. But he had gone, his footsteps mounting the stairs carefully until they went away to the fourth flight and the attics.

Once he was there, Edward put his milk and the hated garibaldi biscuits carefully on the table beside his bed, and went to look out of the window. It was very high. The sky was huge and full of sagging leaden clouds, making the night seem closer than it was by the clock. Ragged jackdaws whirled about on the wind like scraps of torn burned paper. He could see the church tower, the churchyard, the road, and the flat acres of fen with deep dikes criss-crossing them. A small stone bridge. A brick cottage beside a lock, though he did not yet know that was what it was called.

He drank the milk in small sips and wondered what he could do with the biscuits that he could not have swallowed any more than he could have swallowed a live spider. In the end, he opened the cupboard in the wall. It was completely empty. He broke off a corner of the biscuit and crumbled it onto the plate, and climbed up and put the rest far back on the highest shelf he could reach. Perhaps mice would find it. He was not afraid of mice.

And then, as he turned round, he felt something strange, like a rustle of chill across his face, or someone blowing toward him. It was soundless but something in the cupboard caught his eye and he thought that the paper lining the shelves had lifted slightly, as if the movement of air had caught that too.

He went back to the window but it was closed tightly,

and the latch was across. It was the same with the window on the other side. He touched the door but it was closed firmly and it did not move. The room was still again.

FIVE MINUTES LATER, he was in bed, lying flat on his back with the sheet just below his chin, both hands holding it. The wind had got up now. The windows rattled, the sound round the rooftop above him grew louder and then wild, as the gale came roaring across the fen to hit the old house and beat it about the head.

Edward did not remember such a wind but it was outside and could not get in, and so he was not in the least afraid, any more than he was afraid of the sound of rain, or the rattle of hail on a pane. He had left the wall cupboard slightly open but the lining paper did not lift, and there was no chill breeze across his face. This was just weather. This was different.

He went to sleep rocked by the storm, and it howled through his dreams and made him turn over and over in the narrow bed, and in her own room, Kestrel lay troubled by it not for herself, well used to it as she was, but for the boy. At one point when the gale was at its height she almost got up and went to him, but surely, if he were alarmed he would call out, and she felt shy of indicating her feelings or of transmitting alarm. High winds were part of the warp and weft of the place and the old house absorbed them without complaint.

He would get used to them, and when Violet's child came tomorrow, so would she, whatever she was like.

A vision of her sister came into Kestrel's mind as she fell asleep, of the bubble curls and pretty mouth and the coquettish charm she had been mistress of at birth. Leonora. Leonora van Vorst. What sort of a child would Leonora be?

Six

He was sitting on the edge of his bed reading and as he still did not find reading easy, although he loved what he discovered in a book when he found the key to it, he had to concentrate hard and so he did not hear the footsteps on the last flights of uncarpeted stairs or their voices. He read on and one set of footsteps went away again and it was quiet, late afternoon. It had stopped raining, the wind had dropped and there was an uncertain sun on the watery fens.

And then he was aware of her, standing just inside the doorway, and looked up with a start.

"You seem to be very easily frightened," she said.

Edward stared at the girl. She had dark red hair, long and standing out from her head as if she had an electric shock running through her, and dark blue eyes in a china white face.

"I'm not frightened at all."

She smiled a small superior smile and came right into the room to stand a yard or two away from him.

He slid off the bed, remembering manners he had been taught almost from the cradle, and put out his hand.

"I am Edward Cayley," he said. "I suppose you're my cousin Leonora."

She looked at the hand but did not take it.

"How do you do?"

She smiled again, then turned abruptly and went to the window.

"This is a dreadful place," she said. "What are we supposed to do?"

"It isn't actually terrible. It is quiet though."

"Who is that woman?"

"Our aunt. Aunt Kestrel."

Leonora tossed her hair. "The other one, with the sour face."

He smiled. "Mrs. Mullen."

"She doesn't like us."

"Doesn't she?"

"Don't be stupid, can't you tell? But what does it matter?" She looked round his room, summing its contents up quickly, then sat down on the bed.

"Where have you come from?" He opened his mouth to say "London" but she carried on without waiting to hear. "I came from Geneva this time," she said, "but before that from Hong Kong and before that from Rome. Not that way round."

"How did you do that?"

"Well on a ship and a train, of course. I might have flown but it seemed better."

"Not on your own."

"Of course on my own, why not? Did you have to have someone to bring you, like an escort."

"I came in charge of the guard."

"Oh yes, I've done that. I came in charge of stewards and so on." She bounced off the bed. "Your mother's dead."

"I know."

"What did she die of?"

"I'm not sure. No one has ever said."

"Goodness. My mother's alive, so is my father, but somewhere else. At the moment my stepfather is called Claude. I hope he stays, I quite like Claude, but, of course, he won't, they never do for long."

He caught sight of her face then and it was strange and sad and distant.

"We could go out into the garden."

"Why? Is it interesting? I don't expect so. Gardens aren't usually."

"Our aunt found some jigsaw puzzles."

Leonora was at the window.

"Shall I get them out?"

"I don't want to do one but you can."

"No, it's all right. How long did it take you to get here?"

"Two days. I slept on the boat train."

"Were you sick?"

He had gone to stand beside her at the window and he saw that he had made her angry.

"I am never sick. I am an excellent sailor. I suppose you're sick."

"Anyway, it doesn't matter. Some people are, some aren't and you can't die of being sick."

Her eyes seemed to darken and the centers to grow smaller. "Where do you think people go when they die?"

Edward hesitated. He did not know how to behave toward her, whether she wanted to be friendly or hostile, if she was worried about something or about nothing.

"They go to heaven. Or . . . to God."

"Or to hell."

"I'm not sure."

"Hell isn't fire you know."

"Isn't it?"

"Oh no. Hell is a curse. You're forced to wander this world and you can never escape."

"That sounds all right. It's what—you wander this world. You've wandered to all those places."

He could sense something in her that needed reassurance and could not ask for it. He did not know, because he was too young and had never before encountered it, that what he sensed in Leonora was pride. Later, he was to understand, though still without having a word for it.

"Do you remember your mother?"

"No. Aunt Kestrel does but she didn't want to talk about her."

"What, because it might upset you? How could you be upset about a mother you don't remember?"

"No. I think it—it might have upset her."

"Oh."

That was something else he would come to know well, the tone of her voice that signified boredom.

"Tomorrow we'll play a trick on that woman," she said next. "I'll think of something she won't like at all." She sounded so full of a sort of evil glee at the idea that she alarmed him.

"I don't think we ought to do that."

Leonora turned on him in scorn. "Why? Do you want to be her favorite and have her pet you?"

He flushed. "No. I just think it would be a bad thing to do. And mean."

"Of course it would be a bad thing to do. And mean. How silly you are."

"I don't think she's very nice but perhaps it's because she hasn't any children of her own or doesn't know any."

"Aunt Kestrel hasn't any children but she doesn't hate us."

"I don't think Mrs. Mullen would hate us."

"Of course she hates us. And I am going now to think about what trick to play."

"Where are you going?"

But she had already gone. She came and went so silently and completely that he wondered if she did not move at all but simply knew how to just appear and disappear.

He did not see her again until the bell rang for supper and then, just as he was going across the hall, she was there, when she had not been there a second before.

From now on, he determined to watch her.

"Have you thought?"

But Leonora stared at him blankly across the table.

"I wish the weather would improve," Aunt Kestrel

said, slicing a tea-cake and buttering half for each of them. "You would find so many good things to do out of doors."

"What things?"

Aunt Kestrel looked like someone caught out in a lie. That is how Leonora makes me feel, Edward realized, as if she can see through me to my soul and know what I am thinking and if I am telling the truth, or trying to bluff my way out of something.

She had not yet been here for a whole day and already the mood of the house had been changed entirely.

"My mother is said to be the most beautiful woman who has ever lived," Leonora said now. "Did you know that?"

"How ridiculous," Aunt Kestrel said, spluttering out some little droplets of tea. "Of course she is not. Violet was a pretty little girl and grew up to be a pretty woman, though she was helped by clothes and having people to bring out the best in her."

"What people?"

"Oh, hairdressers and . . . you know, those people. But as to being the most beautiful woman who ever lived . . . besides, who could know?"

"It was written in a magazine of fashion." Leonora's face had changed as a blush of annoyance rose through the paleness and her eyes darkened. "It was written under her photograph so it would have to be true. Of course it is true. She is very, very beautiful. She is." Edward watched in horror as Leonora stood up and picked up a small silver cake fork. "She is, she is, she is." As she said it, she stabbed the fork down into the cloth and through to the table, one hard stab for each word. Aunt Kestrel's mouth was half open, her arm slightly outstretched as if she meant to stop the dreadful stabbing, but was unable to make any movement.

"And no one is allowed to say it is not true."

She dropped the fork on the floor and it spun away from her, and then she was gone, the skirt of her blue cotton frock seeming to flick out behind her and then disappear as she disappeared. The door closed slowly of its own accord. Edward sat, wishing that he was able to disappear too but forced to wait for Aunt Kestrel's anger to break over him and take whatever punishment there might be, for them both.

There was none. His aunt sat silent for a moment then said, "I wonder if you can find out what is wrong, Edward?"

He sped to the door. "She is like her mother," she said as he went, but he thought that she was speaking to herself, not to him.

"She is too like her mother."

Seven

He did not see Leonora and the door of her room was shut. He hesitated, listening. The wind had dropped. There was no sound from her and he opened his mouth to say her name, then did not, afraid that her anger was still raging and that she might turn it on him. He thought of the cake fork stabbing into the table.

The house no longer felt strange to him but he did not like it greatly and he was disappointed that his cousin seemed unlikely to become a friend. She was strange, if Iyot House and their Aunt Kestrel were not. She belonged with Mrs. Mullen, he thought, turning on his left side. The last of the light was purple and pale blue in a long thread across the sky, seen through the window opposite his bed. It had not been like this before. Perhaps there would be sun tomorrow and they could explore the world outside. Perhaps things would improve, as in Edward's experience they often did. His school had improved, his eczema had improved, his dog had improved with age after being disobedient and running away all through puppy-hood.

He went to sleep optimistically.

THERE WAS MOONLIGHT and so he could see her when he woke very suddenly.

Leonora was standing in the doorway, her nightgown as white as her skin, her red hair standing out from her head. She was absolutely still, her eyes oddly blank and for several moments Edward thought that she was an apparition. Or a ghost. What was the difference?

"Hello?"

She didn't reply.

"Are you quite all right?"

She did not move. He saw that her feet were bare. Long pale feet. He did not know what to do.

And then she came further into the room, silently on the long pale feet, her hair glowing against the whiteness of her skin and long nightgown.

"Leonora?"

She had walked to the window and was looking out, washed by the moonlight.

Edward got up and went to stand beside her. At first he did not touch her, hardly dared to look directly at her. He had the odd sense that if he did touch her she would feel cold.

"Are you still asleep?"

She turned her head and stared at him out of the blank unseeing eyes.

"You should go back to your own room now. You could hurt yourself."

Stories of people walking out of windows and far from home across fields and into woods while they were deeply asleep came into his mind.

You should not try to wake a sleepwalker, the shock could kill them. You should not touch a sleepwalker, or they may stay that way and never wake again.

He began to panic when Leonora sat on the ledge and started to undo the window latch, and then he did reach out and touch her shoulder. She stopped but did not look at him.

"Come on. We're going back now."

He nudged her gently and she got up and let him guide her out of his room and back to her own. He steered her to the bed, pulled back the covers and she climbed in obediently, and turned on her side. Her eyes closed. Edward spread the covers over her with care and watched her until he was sure she was fully asleep, then crept out.

Eight

"Oh do hurry up, hurry up . . ."

Aunt Kestrel came into the hall. "If you are going out you need stout shoes. The grass is very wet."

Leonora ignored her, hand on the front door.

Edward looked at his feet. Were the shoes "stout"?

"Well, perhaps you'll be all right. Don't go too far."

"Hurry up," Leonora said again. The inner door opened and she went to the heavy outer one, which had a large iron key and a bolt and chain.

"Anyone would suppose ravening beasts and high-waymen would be wanting to burst in," she said, laughing a small laugh.

Mrs. Mullen was in the dark recesses of the hall watching, lips pinched together.

Aunt Kestrel sighed as she closed both doors. She was confused by the children, and bewildered. Leonora was like Violet, which boded ill though perhaps not in quite the same way, who knew? Edward was simply opaque. Had they taken to one another? Were they settling?

She went into her sitting room with the morning paper.

Mrs. Mullen did not ask the same questions because she had made up her mind from seeing both children, Edward, the little namby-pamby, too sweet-tongued to trust, and Leonora. She had looked into Leonora's eyes when she had first arrived, and seen the devil there and her judgment was made and snapped shut on the instant.

᠕

"WHERE ARE YOU going?" Edward watched his cousin going to the double gates. "The garden is on this side."

Leonora gave her usual short laugh. "Who wants to go in a garden?"

She lifted the latch of a small gate within the gate and stepped through. He went after her because he thought he should look after her and persuade her to come back, but by the time he had clambered over the bottom strut she was walking fast down the road and a minute later, had crossed it and started up the path that led to the open fens.

"Leonora, we'd better not . . ."

She tossed her red hair and went on.

When he caught her up she was standing on the bank looking down into the river. It was inky and slick and ran quite slowly.

"Be careful."

"Can you swim?"

"No, can you?"

"I wonder what you can do. Of course I can swim, one of my stepfathers taught me in . . . I think it was Italy."

"How many have you had? Stepfathers?"

She did not answer, but moved away and followed a rivulet that led away from the main course deep into the fen. They looked back. Iyot House reared up, higher than the other huddled houses, dark behind its trees. The church rose like a small ship toward the west.

It was very still, not cold. The reeds stood like guardsmen.

"Where are we going?"

"Anywhere."

But it was only a little further on when she stopped again. The rivulet had petered out and widened to form a pool, which reflected the sky, the clouds which were barely moving.

"There might be newts here," Edward said.

"Are they like lizards?"

"I think so."

"There are lizards everywhere in hot countries. On stones. On walls. They slither into the cracks. Are you afraid of things like that?"

"I've never seen one."

She faced him, her eyes challenging, dark as sloes in her face.

"Are you afraid of hell? Or snakes or mad bulls or fire coming out of people's mouths?"

Edward laughed.

"You should be careful," she said softly. "Mind what you laugh at. See if there are any of your newt things in there."

They bent over and, instinctively, Edward reached out to take her hand in case she went too near to the edge. Leonora snatched it away as if his own had burned her, making him almost lose his balance.

"Don't you ever dare to do that again."

He wanted to weep with frustration at this girl who made him feel stupid, and so as not to show his face to her, he knelt down and stared into the water, trying hopelessly to see newts, or frogs—any living, moving creature.

"Oh. How strange."

Leonora was pointing to the smooth, still surface of the water. At first, Edward could not see anything except the sky, which now had patches of blue behind the white clouds. He looked harder and saw what he thought was—must be—Leonora's face reflected in the water, and there was his own, wavery but recognizably him.

Leonora's red hair spread out in the water like weed, and the collar of her blue frock was clear, and a little of her long pale neck. But her face was not the same. Or rather, it was the same but . . .

"Oh," he said.

"Who is it?" Leonora whispered.

He could not tell her. He could not say, because he did not really know, who he saw or what. He reached out his hand to her and she held it fast in her own, so tight that it seemed to hurt his bones.

"What is it? What can you see?"

She went on staring, still gripping his hand, but even when he bent down, Edward could only make out the blurred reflection of both their faces upside down. There was nothing behind them and you could not see below.

"You're hurting my hand."

And then, she was scrabbling in the earth for small stones, and clods of turf, and then larger stones. She threw them into the water and then hurled the largest one and their images splintered and the water rocked and in a moment, stilled again and there they were, the boy Edward, the girl Leonora. Nothing else.

"I don't understand," Edward said. But she had gone, racing away from him along the path. He watched her, troubled, but he knew he ought not to let her be by herself, sensing that she was quixotic and unsafe, and followed her from a distance but always keeping her in sight as she ran in the direction of Iyot Church.

Nine

"What did you see?" Edward asked.

He had found her wandering round the side aisles looking at memorial tablets set into the walls and brasses into the floor, running her hand over the carved pew ends and the steps of the pulpit, lifting the hassocks off their hooks and dropping them onto the pews, going restlessly, pointlessly from one to the other.

She did not answer. He was worried, felt responsible.

"I think we should go now. Maybe we aren't allowed in here at all."

Leonora came to his side, smiling. "What do you think would happen to us?"

"We'd get into trouble."

"Who from?"

"The parson."

She shook her head. Her hair lifted and seemed to float out from her head, then settle back.

"God?"

"Or the devil."

"Why would the devil care? It isn't his place."

"Do you believe in them?"

"Of course I do," Edward said. "Look—that is God, in that window."

"And there is the devil, at the bottom of that picture." Her voice was scornful.

"No, that's a snake."

"The devil is a serpent, which is what a snake is in the Bible. I know a lot about it."

"I still think we should go."

But before he could move, Leonora had taken hold of his hand again and was pressing her fingernails into the palm. She was staring at a large silver plate that stood on a dark wooden chest against the wall beside them.

"What's the matter? I think it's for collecting money. You know, when they go round."

But she seemed not to hear him, only went on looking at the shining circle, her face pale as paper, eyes coal-dark.

He got up and went to the dish. His own face reflected shimmering in the surface though it was distorted and hard to make out.

"Don't look," Leonora said. "Move away from it, don't look."

"Why? It isn't dangerous."

He was about to bend right over and put his face very close to the silver, when Leonora leaped up, lifted the plate and hurled it away from her down the aisle.

It crashed against the stone flags and then went rolling crazily until it spun and fell flat in a corner.

"Why did you do that?"

But she was gone again, out of the church, leaving the door wide open, and away down the path before jumping off between two high gravestones. The wind had got up again and was bending the tall uncut grasses and the branches of the yew.

This time, Edward did not race after her. He was tired of what he decided was some sort of game which she would not explain to him and in which he had no part, but he also thought that she was trying to frighten him and he was not going to allow it.

He came slowly out of the church and down the path to the gate. Then he looked round but could not see her. She had gone back to the house then. He would see her racing down the road.

As he put his hand on the gate, the heavy wooden door of the church banged loudly shut behind him in the wind.

Leonora was nowhere ahead. He turned, and then caught a glimpse of her, low down behind the stone wall among the gravestones. The wind caught the edge of her blue frock and lifted it a little.

"Leonora . . ."

What he saw on her face when she glanced round was a look so full of malice and evil, so twisted and distorted with dislike and scorn and a sort of laughing hatred, that he wanted to be the one to run, to get away as fast as he could, back to what he now thought of as the safety and shelter of Iyot House. But as long as she looked at him, he could not move, his limbs, his body, even his breath, seemed to be paralyzed. He could not even cry out or speak because his lungs and his mouth felt full of heavy sand. Her look lasted for hours, for years; he was struck dumb and motionless for a lifetime, while Leonora held his gaze.

But he was just as suddenly free and light as air and full of almost electric energy, and he ran.

The hands of the clock on the church tower had not moved.

❧

FOR THE REST of that day and several days more they fell under the spell of Bagatelle, after Aunt Kestrel had unearthed the old set and taught the game to them.

❧

"AND IF YOU grow tired of that, here are the cards. I will teach you Piquet."

But they did not grow tired. The weather changed and became hot, with clear, blue skies that paled to white on the horizon and a baking sun. The streams dried, the pond was lower, the river ran sluggishly. The air smelled of heat, heat seemed to fill their mouths and scratch at their eyes. They went into the garden under the shade of a huge copper beech and set the Bagatelle board out on an old table. Mrs. Mullen brought a jug of lukewarm lemon barley and the despised garibaldi biscuits and they played game after game, mainly in silence. At first,

Leonora won. She was quicker and slyer and saw her chances. Edward was cautious and steady. At home he played chess with his half-brother.

There was a small fish pond over which dragonflies hovered, their blue sheen catching the sun, and the flower beds were seething with bees.

"At last," Aunt Kestrel said, as Mrs. Mullen brought in her coffee. "They have settled down together perfectly well."

Mrs. Mullen went to the window and saw the table, the game, the boy and girl bent over the board, one fair head, one brilliant red. She mistrusted the girl and thought the boy a namby-pamby. Either way, having children to stay in the house had not altered her opinion, except to harden it against them.

"I agree with you that Leonora behaved very badly, but we have to forgive her. It is all so strange and odd for them. Don't bear a grudge, Mrs. Mullen."

After the housekeeper had gone out of the room, Kestrel sat thinking about her, wondering why she was so very hostile, so clearly unable to warm to either child in any way, so readily seeing the bad and fearing worse. She knew little of her background and former life, other than that she had no children and her husband worked as a bargeman. Why she was so embittered she could not fathom.

꒰

THE HEAT CONTINUED until the air grew stale and every morning was more oppressive than the last. The sun filmed over with a haze and midges jazzed above the waterways.

"Time we had a storm," Aunt Kestrel said over supper at the beginning of the third week of heat.

Edward looked apprehensive. Leonora, on the other side of the table, saw his face and frowned. The previous day he had beaten her three times at Bagatelle and now she played with an angry concentration, determined to win and breathless with silent fury when, time after time, she did not.

The heat formed a heavy cloud that hung low over the garden, obscuring any sun. Edward's skin itched inside his clothes.

"Let's stop."

"No. I have to win first."

"You can win another time. It's too hot."

"Stupid. I said I want to win first, then we can stop."

"You might not win for another ten games. I'm going to read indoors by the window."

In a single flash of movement, Leonora stood up, overturned the Bagatelle board, sending it flying onto the grass and scattering its pieces, and then she screamed, a terrible, violent scream, so loud that Edward ran from her and from the awful sound of it, across the garden, up the steps and into the house, slamming the heavy door behind him.

Mrs. Mullen was in the shadows of the hall, making him start.

"I said everything would be turned upside down and we would have nothing but upset and disturbance, but never did I expect what came here."

Edward dared not move.

"Listen to it."

She was still screaming without apparently needing to pause for breath.

"It will turn you as well. In the end, there'll be not a pin to put between you. Can you not feel it?"

"Feel it?" Edward could scarcely hear his own voice speaking into the dark hall.

"What possesses her? Can you not feel it creeping over you too? No child could come within sight of her and not be turned." She came out of the shadows and went smartly to the door, turned the key and slid the bolt.

"What are you doing?"

"Shutting the door against her," Mrs. Mullen said. "Now you get off upstairs out of the sight and sound of her while you've a chance."

"But how will she get in?"

"Maybe she won't and that would be no bad thing." She left him.

For several minutes, Edward stood wondering what he should do but in the end, after listening for any sound of Mrs. Mullen's return, he went to the drawing room, in which they had only been allowed to step once and where there were French windows opening onto the side terrace and the wide stone steps to the garden below. The air was sultry, the sky gathering into a yellowish mass like a boil over the house. He went to where they had been sitting earlier. The Bagatelle was still scattered over the grass and the table upturned.

"Ah, she's sent the good little boy to tidy up." He spun round. Leonora had appeared from nowhere and was standing a few yards from him.

"I came to find you. She locked the door to keep you out but she shouldn't have done that. I think there is going to be a storm."

"Are you frightened of storms?"

"No. But you might have been."

Leonora laughed the dry little laugh. "I'm not afraid of anything at all."

"You were frightened of something. You were frightened of something down in the water."

She lunged forward, grabbed his arm and bent it backward so that he cried out. "You must never ever say that again and I didn't see anything and I was not afraid. I am never afraid. Say it. 'Leonora is never afraid.'" She twisted his arm a little further back.

"Leonora is never afraid let go of my arm you're hurting."

"Manners, little boy. 'Please.'"

"Please."

She almost tossed his arm away from her, turned and went round to the side of the house. Edward followed her, angry that he had bothered to worry about her and feel worried enough to come and find her.

She ran up the steps, and through the French windows which he had left ajar, but as he came up behind her, shut them quickly and turned the key. Then she stood, her face close to the glass, looking out at him, smiling.

Ten

Edward woke when his room flared white and then for a split second, vivid blue. The thunder came almost simultaneously, seeming to crack the attic roof open like an axe splitting a log. He sat up watching it through the curtainless window for a while, until hail spattered so fiercely onto the glass that sudden light and sudden dark were all he could see. He lay down and listened. He had been two or three years old when his half-brother had taken him on a boat and out to sea; they had huddled together in the small cabin as a storm flared and crashed all round them. His brother had been bright-eyed with excitement and Edward had sensed that this was something to revel in, knowing no danger, only the drama and heightened atmosphere. He had loved storms from then, though there had never been one so momentous. Now, this was almost as good, vast and overpowering across the fens and around Iyot House.

The lightning flickered vividly across the sky again and in the flash, he saw Leonora standing in the doorway of his room, her eyes wide, face stark white.

Edward sat up. "It's amazing! I love storms."

She went to his window. "Yes." She spoke in a whisper, as if she were afraid speaking aloud might change it.

Edward got up and stood beside her.

"You should see the storms in the East. A storm across the water in Hong Kong. A storm over the mountains. They race through your blood, such storms."

HE UNDERSTOOD HER at once and for the first time they shared something completely, bound up together in the excitement and pleasure of the storm, so that he clasped hold of her hand when a thunderclap made the house shake and the walls of the attics shudder and her nails dug into his palm at a blue-green zigzag of lightning.

"I thought you would be crying," Leonora said, glancing at him sideways.

"Oh no, oh no!"

"We could go out."

"Don't be silly, it's like a monsoon, we'd be soaked in a minute."

"Have you been in a monsoon? I have. The earth steams and you could boil a pan of water on the ground. It brings down whole trees."

"I want to go there."

They were linked in a passion to soar from this storm to that one.

"My mother is there now," Leonora said.

"Where? In a monsoon?"

"In India, I think. Or Burma. Or perhaps she is back in Hong Kong. They move about so."

He was unsure whether to be envious or sorry for her.

"When will she come back for you?"

Leonora shrugged and flicked her hair about her shoulders. The storm was receding, the lightning moving away to the east and the sea, the rain easing to a steady, dull downpour.

"I hope she'll come before too long," Edward said. "You must miss her very much."

"I don't," Leonora said, "and I don't." And sailed out of the room on her bare and silent feet.

THE NEXT MORNING, the parcels began to arrive. There were two, one very large, one small, and after that, as the post from abroad caught up, one or two almost every day. Leonora took them upstairs, ignoring the remarks made by Mrs. Mullen about spoiled children and the concern of Aunt Kestrel that perhaps some should be put away until later.

"They are my parcels," she said, dragging a heavy one behind her, refusing help.

"But you," she said to Edward, "may look if you like."

MOST OF THE parcels contained clothes, few of which fitted, dresses made of bright silk embroidered with gold thread and decorated with little mirrors, trailing fine scarves and long skirts with several floating panels. Leonora glanced at each one, held it up to herself, then tossed it away, to fall on the floor or her bed. Once or twice she put on a scarf and twirled round in it and kept it on. There were silver boxes and carved wooden animals, brass bells and on one day a huge box of pale green and pink Turkish delight that smelled of scent and sent a puff of white sugar into the air when she lifted the wooden lid. They ate several pieces, one small, sticky bite at a time, and the intense sweetness set their teeth on edge.

"My mother never sends what I really want. She just doesn't."

"But the sweets are nice. What do you really want?"

"One thing."

"What thing?"

"And she knows and she never sends it."

"When is your birthday?"

"August the tenth; I am a Leo."

"That is quite soon. So I think she is going to send it for then."

Leonora ripped open the thin brown paper on her last parcel. It contained a black satin cushion covered in gold and silver beads.

"How horrible, horrible, *horrible*." The cushion bumped against the far wall and fell.

Edward wiped the sugar powder off his mouth. "What is it that you do really want?"

"A doll," Leonora said. "You would think she could easily send me a doll but she never, never, never does. I hate my mother."

"No, you should never say that."

"Why? I do."

"No."

"Why?"

"Because—you just shouldn't."

"You don't know anything about it. You don't know anything about mothers because you haven't got one."

"I know," Edward said. "But I did once have one."

"If she sent me what I wanted I would be able to love her."

He wondered if that could be true, that someone made you love them by giving you what you wanted, or, that you would not love them until they did. It was confusing.

"I think that she will send you a doll. I think you will get it on your birthday."

BUT THE BIRTHDAY came and she did not.

Aunt Kestrel gave her an ivory carved chess set in a wooden casket, a set of hairbrushes and a jar of sweets, which she had handed to Edward the night before, to hand over as from himself. Leonora's face had been pinched and sallow and when she had taken her things upstairs, with the handkerchief embroidered with her initial from Mrs. Mullen, Edward had gone into their aunt's sitting room.

"She doesn't mean to be ungrateful."

"No. It is hard to know what to give but I thought you might teach her chess as you are so fond of it." The Bagatelle board had been damaged beyond repair by being left outside in the storm.

"Yes. It is her mother."

Aunt Kestrel sighed.

"She sends her so many parcels with nice things but never what she really wants."

"The trouble is, Violet barely knows her own child and always had more interest in herself than anyone else. You will please never repeat that, Edward."

"No."

He explained about the doll.

"It seems an obvious thing to send. But I am going to London next week. If Violet has not had the sense to send a doll, I must find one."

Eleven

Another storm was building for the whole day Aunt Kestrel was away. The fen was dun green with the river like an oil slick where it ran deep between its banks. Edward watched the lock keeper pace slowly along, peering into the water, cross the bridge, then walk back. The thunder rumbled round the edges of the sky.

Leonora was sullen and silent, not wanting to learn chess, not wanting to have him anywhere near her. In the end, he found a book about adventures in the diamond mines of South Africa, and read it sitting on the windowsill. Mrs. Mullen rang them down for lunch, which was cold beef, cold potatoes and hard boiled eggs, with custard to follow, and they ate it silently in the dining room as the rain began to teem down the windows.

Mrs. Mullen did not come near to them for the rest of the day. She rang the supper bell, told them they must be in bed by eight o'clock, and disappeared behind her door.

Eight came and the attics were pitch dark. The storm had fizzled out but the rain was so loud they could not hear themselves speak, but did a jigsaw in silence. Leonora was bored and lost interest. Edward went to bed and read his book. He was not unhappy at Iyot House. He was a boy of equable temperament and no strong passions, who was never seriously unhappy anywhere, but tonight, he wished strongly that he could be at home in his own London bed. How long he and Leonora were staying here no one had said.

He usually slept deeply and dreamed little, but tonight, he fell into a restless, uncomfortable doze, skidding along the surface of strange dreams and hearing sounds that half woke him. He had an odd sense that something was about to happen, as if Iyot House and everyone in it were a bubbling pan about to boil over and hiss out onto a stove. In the middle of the night, he woke yet again, to the sound of crying, but it was not coming from his cousin's room, it came from somewhere near at hand and the crying was of a baby not a girl like Leonora.

He sat up. Everything was still. There was very little wind but clouds slid in front of a full moon now and again.

Nothing stirred. No one cried.

He lay down again but the strange sensation of foreboding did not leave him, even in sleep.

And then, a different sort of crying woke him, and this time he recognized it.

HE WENT TO Leonora. She had her head half underneath her pillow, which lifted and fell occasionally.

"It's all right."

He pretended not to hear her when she told him to go away. It had been a miserable birthday and he was sorry for her.

"I want you to tell me something."

She flung her pillow off her face. "I said to . . ."

"I know but I'm not going to. I want you to tell me."

Leonora turned her back on him.

"What kind of doll would you like best? I want you to tell me what it would look like, tell me everything."

"Why? You can't get it for me so why would I tell you?"

"I can't get it for you but I can do something else."

Silence. Then she sat up and pushed her hair out of her eyes. Edward was careful not to stare at her.

"I've got paper and some pencils and paints and I can draw it for you."

She made a scornful sound in her throat.

"Isn't it better than no doll? And Aunt Kestrel is bringing you one."

"She wouldn't find anything like this."

"But she will find something nice."

SHE DESCRIBED THE doll she wanted very well, so that Edward could draw and then paint it with the greatest care. It was an Indian royal bride, with elaborate clothes and jewels and braiding in her hair, which

Leonora knew in every tiny detail, every color and shading and texture.

"Have you wanted one like it for a very long time?"

"Since I was about two or three. It is the only thing I ever ever wanted and my mother knows that and she has never got it for me."

"Perhaps she tried hard and couldn't. Perhaps there has never been one like it in any shop."

"Of course there hasn't, she should have had it made for me."

He went on painting the doll, wondering as he did so why Leonora did not know that it was impolite to demand and want and order presents.

"I think it's finished but I shall put it here to dry."

HE WAS AFRAID to wait until she had looked at it and went back quietly to bed, and slept at once.

The following morning, he went by himself out to the garden early, before breakfast. Leonora did not follow him for a long time but eventually she came, carrying the picture he had painted.

"I'm sorry it's not a doll," Edward said.

"Yes. But there will be a doll. Just exactly like this. I know there will."

She put the painting down on the grass. She had not thanked him for it and he was not very surprised that she left it there when they had to run in from the heavy rain.

SHE ASKED A hundred times when Aunt Kestrel would be back from London. Mrs. Mullen said, "When she's ready." Edward said cautiously that it might be after they were asleep.

"I won't go to sleep until I see the doll."

✂

SHE DID NOT. It was after eleven o'clock when she woke Edward to say that she had heard the station taxi.

"Get up, get up, I'm going downstairs."

Her eyes were wild with excitement and she had two small spots of color burning in the pale of her face. She raced down the stairs so fast he was afraid she would trip but her feet seemed not to touch the ground. She burst into Aunt Kestrel's sitting room but then some sense of how to behave touched her enough to make her stop and say, "I am sorry. I should have knocked on the door." But her eyes had traveled straight to a large box, wrapped in brown paper, on the round table.

"You should both be in bed. It is very very late."

Edward was about to defend his cousin by pointing out that she should be excused because she was so excited about her birthday present, but Leonora had already gone to the table and put her hand on the box.

"Is this for me, is this it?"

There was a silence. Kestrel was tired, and wanted only to give the child her present and have them all go to bed but she saw Violet in the greedy little face, a carelessness about anyone or anything except herself, let alone even the most ordinary politeness. She knew that she ought to reprimand, to withhold the box until the next morning, to start however belatedly to control this strange, proud, self-centered child to whom she felt she had a vague responsibility.

But this was not the time and besides, she could not face whatever scene might follow.

"Yes, you may open it but after that you must go to bed or you will make yourself overwrought and ill."

Leonora gave her a swift, ecstatic smile and then started to open the parcel but the string had difficult knots, so that Aunt Kestrel was obliged to find her small scissors. The child's eyes did not leave the parcel. Edward held his breath. He prayed for the doll to be like the one he had painted for her, as like as possible and if not, then every bit as grand.

The doll was in a plain oblong white box, tied with red ribbon. Now Leonora held her breath too, her small fingers trembling as she unpicked the bow. Edward moved closer, wanting to see, wanting to close his eyes.

THERE WAS THE rustle of layer after layer of tissue paper as she unwrapped each sheet very carefully. And then she came to the doll.

It was a baby doll, large and made of china, with staring blue eyes and a rosebud mouth in a smooth, expressionless face. It wore a white cotton nightdress and beside it was a glass feeding bottle.

Neither Edward nor Kestrel ever forgot the next

moments. Leonora looked at the doll, her body rigid, her hands clenched. Then, with what sounded like a growl which rose in pitch from deep in her throat into her mouth and became a dreadful animal howl, she lifted it out of the box, turned and hurled it at the huge marble fireplace. It hit a carved pillar and there was a crack as it fell, one large piece and a few shards broken from the head to leave a jagged hollow, so that in his shock Edward wondered crazily if brains and blood might spill out and spread over the hearth tiles.

There was a silence so absolute and terrible that it seemed anything might have happened next, the house split down the middle or the ground open into a fiery pit, or one of them to drop down dead.

Twelve

Leonora ran. Her footsteps went thundering up the stairs and they could hear them, even louder, even faster, as she reached the top flights. The door of her bedroom slammed shut.

Aunt Kestrel seemed to have difficulty catching her breath and at last Edward said, "I'm sure she didn't mean to be hurtful."

She looked at him out of eyes whose centers were like brilliant pin-points of light but said nothing. Edward went to the doll in the hearth, picked it up, together with the broken pieces of china head, and trailed out, afraid to speak, even to glance at Aunt Kestrel.

THE ATTIC FLOOR was dark and silent. He hesitated at Leonora's door and listened. She must have heard him come upstairs and stop and did not want to see him. He went into his own room, carrying the doll, switched his bedside lamp on and sat down with it on his bed. The single large piece of china from its damaged head could probably be glued back, but the shards and fragments he thought were far too small. He sat holding it, wondering what he could do.

"Poor Dolly," he said, holding it in his arms, rocking and stroking it.

The doll stared blankly, the crevasse in its china skull jagged, with cracks now running from it down the face like the spider cracks in walls. But he was bleary with tiredness and returned the doll to its box, put the lid back on and pushed it under his bed.

ᙏ

HE SLEPT RESTLESSLY, as if he had a fever, hearing the crack of the china doll hitting the fireplace and seeing Leonora's twisted, furious little face as she hurled it, and the wind howling through a crack in the window frame mingled with her scream. It was not yet midnight by his small traveling clock when he woke again. The wind still howled but in between he heard something else, fainter, and not so alarming.

He went out onto the landing. The wind was muffled and now that he heard it more clearly he thought it was the sound of Leonora's crying. Her door was closed. Edward put his ear close to the wood. Silence. He waited. Still silence. He turned the handle slowly and eased open the door a very little. He could hear Leonora's very soft breathing but nothing else, no sobbing, no snuffling, nothing at all to show that she was crying now or had just been crying.

He could not go back to sleep, because of the wind and remembering the scene earlier, and because, when he lay down, he could hear the faint sound again. It was coming from beneath his bed, where the doll lay in its box. He sat bolt upright and shook his head to and fro hard to clear the sound but it had not gone away when he stopped. The wind was dying down and before long it died altogether and then his room was frighteningly silent except for the crying.

He was not a cowardly boy, though he had a natural cautiousness, but for a long time he lay, not daring to lean over and pull the box out from under the bed. He had no doubt that the sound came from it and he knew that he was awake, no longer in the middle of a nightmare, and that a china doll could not cry.

The crying went on.

WHEN HE GATHERED enough courage to open the box, taking the lid off slowly and moving each layer of tissue paper round the doll with great caution, he looked at the broken face and saw nothing, no fresh cracks or marks and above all, no tears and no changed expression to one of sadness or distress. The doll still stared out sightlessly and when he touched it the china was cold as cold.

He waited. Nothing. He covered the doll and moved

it back out of sight. He lay down. The soft crying began again at once.

Edward got out of bed and switched on his lamp, took the box and without opening it again, carried it over to the deep cupboard and climbed onto a wooden stool. He put the box on the top shelf and pushed it as far to the back as he could, into the pitch darkness and dust.

"Now be quiet," he said, "please stop crying and be quiet."

He lay still for a long time, his ears straining to hear the faintest sound from the cupboard. But there was none. The doll was silent.

Thirteen

For the next three nights the doll cried until Aunt Kestrel asked Edward why he was white-faced with dark stains beneath his eyes, from lack of sleep. He said nothing to anyone and Leonora had spent little time with him. She had been in disgrace, forbidden to go outside, forbidden to have toys, kept to her room until she gave what Aunt Kestrel called "a heartfelt apology." Edward had crept in a couple of times and found her sitting staring out of the window, or lying on her back on the bed, not reading, not sleeping, just looking up at the ceiling. He had offered to stay, told her he was sorry, that he would ask Aunt Kestrel to let her come outside, suggested this or that he could bring to her. She had either not replied or shaken her head, but once, she had looked at him and said, "Mrs. Mullen said I was possessed by a demon. I think that may be true."

He had told her demons did not exist, that she simply had a bad temper and would learn to overcome it, but she said it was not just a bad temper, it was an evil one.

Mrs. Mullen had brought her boiled fish, peas and a glass of water on a tray and told her she was bringing badness upon the house.

"I am, I am."

"Don't be silly. I'm very bored. I wish you would apologize and then you could come out and we could do something, walk along the river and watch the lock open or look for herons."

But she had yawned and turned away.

❧

THE DOLL CRIED for a fourth night and this time he climbed up to the shelf and took it down. It lay in its box, stiff and still, looking like a body in a coffin.

And realizing that, he knew what he should do.

❧

HE WAS SURE he should do it by himself. Leonora was likely to scream or have a fright, behave stupidly or tell Aunt Kestrel. The prospect only frightened him a little.

Leonora was allowed downstairs, though because she had stood in front of Aunt Kestrel with a mutinous face and refused to apologize, she was still forbidden the outside world.

❧

IT WAS HOT again, the sun blazing out of an enamel blue sky, the fens baked and the channels running dry but when Edward woke at five the air still had a morning damp and freshness. He dressed in shorts and shirt, and put on his plimsolls which made no noise.

He looked in the box. Dolly lay still in her tissue paper shroud, though he had heard the crying as he went to sleep and when he woke once in the night.

Someone would hear him, the stairs would creak, the door key would make a clink, the door would stick, as it did after rain. He waited, holding his breath, for Mrs. Mullen to appear and ask what he was doing, or Aunt Kestrel to take the box and order him back to bed.

But he went stealthily, made no sound. No one heard him, no one came.

❧

THE ROAD TO the church was dusty under the early morning sun. Smoke curled from the chimney of the lock keeper's cottage beside the water. The dog barked. A heron rose from the river close beside him, a great pale ghost flapping away low over the fen.

He was afraid of the churchyard, afraid of the gnarled trunks of the yew trees and the soft swish of tall grasses against his legs. At the back, against the wall, the gravestones were half sunken into the earth, their stone lettering too worn away or moss-covered to read. No one left flowers here, no one cleared and tidied. No one remembered these ancient dead. He wondered about what was under the soil and inside the coffins, imagined skulls and bones stretched out.

He had brought a tin spade he had found in a cup-

board. Its edge was rough and the wooden handle wob-
bled in its shaft and when he started trying to dig with
it into the tussocks of grass he realized it would break
before he had broken into the ground. But further along
the grass petered out to thin soil and pine needles and
using the spade and his hands, he dug out enough. It
took a long time. His hands blistered quickly and the
blisters split open and his arms tired. A thrush came and
pecked at the soil he had uncovered and a wagon went
down the road. He ducked behind the broad tree trunk.

When he came to bury the doll in its small cardboard
coffin he thought he should say a prayer, as people
always did at funerals, but it was not easy to think of
suitable words.

"Oh God, let Dolly lie in peace without crying."

He bowed his head. The thrush went on pecking at
the soil, even after he had dragged it over the coffin and
the grave with his tin spade.

🙝

WHEN HE SLIPPED back into the house, he heard Mrs.
Mullen from the kitchen, and his aunt moving about her
room. It was after seven o'clock.

🙝

NO ONE FOUND out. No one took the slightest notice
of him, he was of no account. A telegram had arrived
saying that Leonora's mother was in London and wait-

ing for her, she should be put on the train as soon as possible that day.

"I long for her," Aunt Kestrel said, as she finished reading the telegram out.

Mrs. Mullen, setting down the silver pot of coffee on its stand, made a derisive sound under her breath.

☙

THE MORNING WAS a scramble of boxes and trunks and people flying up and down the stairs. Edward went outside, afraid to be told that he was getting underfoot, the image of the silent, buried doll filling his mind. He did not know what he might do if Leonora asked for it.

She did not. She stood in the hall surrounded by her luggage, her hair tied back in a ribbon which made her look unfamiliar, already someone he did not know. He could not picture where she was going to, or imagine her mother and the latest stepfather.

"I will probably never see you again," she said. The station taxi was at the door and Aunt Kestrel was putting on her hat, looking in her bag. She would see Leonora onto the train.

"You might," Edward said. "We are cousins."

"No. Our mothers hated one another. I think we will be strangers."

She put out a slender, cool hand and he shook it. He wanted to say something more, remind her of things they had said to one another, what had happened, what they had shared, to hold on to this strange, interesting holiday. But Leonora was already somewhere else and he sensed that she would not welcome such reminders.

He watched her walk, stiff-backed, down the path, her luggage stowed away in the taxi, Aunt Kestrel fussing behind her.

"Goodbye, Leonora," he said quietly.

She did not look round, only climbed into the taxi and sat staring straight ahead as the car moved off. She did not glance back at him, or at Iyot House, which he understood was for her already part of the past and moving farther and farther away as the taxi wheels turned.

The sound of the motor died away.

"And good riddance," Mrs. Mullen said from the hall. "That's a bad one and brought nothing but bad with her, so be glad she's gone and pray she's left none of it behind her."

EDWARD WOKE IN the middle of the night to a deathly stillness, in the house and outside, and remembered that he was alone in the attics. Aunt Kestrel was two floors below, Mrs. Mullen in the basement. Leonora had gone.

He closed his eyes and tried to picture a sea of black velvet, which he had once been told was the way to bring on sleep, and after a time he did fall into drowsiness, but through it, in the distance, he heard the sound of paper rustling and the muffled crying of Dolly, buried beneath the earth.

PART THREE

Fourteen

I was abroad when I had the letter telling of my Aunt
Kestrel's death. She was over ninety and had been in a
nursing home and failing for some time. I had always
sent her birthday and Christmas cards and presents but
I had seen her very little since the holidays I spent at Iyot
as a boy and now, as one always does, I felt guilty that I
had not made more effort to visit her in her old age. I am
sure she must have been lonely. She was an intelligent
woman with many interests and one who was happy in
her own company. She was not a natural companion for
a small boy but she had always done her best to ensure
that I was happy when I stayed there and as I grew older
I had been able to talk to her more about the things
that interested her and which I was beginning to learn
a little about—medieval history, military biography, the
Fenlands, and her impeccable botanical illustrating.

I was saddened by her death and planned to return

for her funeral but the day after I received the news, I had a letter from her solicitor informing me that Aunt Kestrel had given him strict and clear instructions that it was to be entirely private, followed by cremation, and so anxious had she been not to have any mourners that the day and time were being kept from everyone save those immediately involved and the lawyer himself. But he concluded:

"However, I have Mrs. Dickinson's instructions that she wishes you and your cousin, Mrs. Leonora Sebastian to attend my office, on a day to be arranged to your convenience, to be told the contents of her Will, of which I am the executor."

I WROTE TO Leonora at the last address I had but I had had no contact with her for some years. I knew that she had married and been divorced and thought she sounded like her mother's daughter, but she had not replied to my last two cards and had apparently dropped out of sight.

Then, the evening I received the solicitor's letter, she telephoned me. I had just arrived back in London. She sounded as I might have expected, haughty and somewhat brusque.

"I suppose this is necessary, Edward? It's not convenient and I hate those bloody fens."

"He wouldn't have asked us if he could have dealt with it any other way—he is almost certainly acting on

Aunt Kestrel's instructions. I shall drive up. Would you like me to take you?"

"No, I'm not sure what arrangements I shall make. I want to see the house, do you? I presume we are the only legatees and we'll get everything? Though as I am older and my mother was older than yours, it would seem fairer that I get the lion's share."

She left me speechless. We agreed to meet at Iyot House, and then again at the solicitor's the following morning. I wondered what she would look like now, whether she still had the wonderful flaring red hair, if she still had a temper, if she had married again and borne any children. I knew almost nothing about Leonora's adult life, as I imagined she knew little about mine. She would not have had enough interest in me to find out.

She had not, of course, turned up the previous evening at the house, and left no message. I daresay she couldn't be bothered. But that she would bother to attend the reading of our aunt's will I had no doubt.

Fifteen

The solicitor's office was everything one would have expected, housed in a small building in the Market Square of Cold Eeyle, which was probably Elizabethan and little changed, but the solicitor himself, a Mr. James Maundeville, was quite unlike the person I had pictured. He had worked for his father and uncle, and then taken over the firm when both had retired. He was only in his late thirties, at a guess, and had a woman as junior partner.

"Mrs. Sebastian is not here yet. Can I get you some coffee or would you prefer to wait until she arrives?"

I said that I would wait and we chatted about my aunt and Iyot House, while we looked out onto the square, which was small, with shops and banks and businesses on two sides, the Town Hall and an open cobbled market on the other. It was a cold, windy morning with clouds scudding past the rooftops, but the fog had quite gone.

We chatted for perhaps ten minutes, and then Maundeville went out, saying he had something to sign. Another ten minutes went by. I was not surprised. It fitted in with everything I had known of Leonora that she should be so late and it was forty minutes after ten when I finally heard voices and footsteps on the stairs. Maundeville's secretary opened the door and said that he was on the telephone, apologized, and said that she would bring coffee in a couple of minutes.

I HAD WONDERED how much my cousin might have changed but as she walked into the room, I knew her at once. Her flaring red hair had softened in color a little, but still sprang from her head in the old, commanding way; her face was as pale, though now made up and with a tautness at the sides of her eyes and jaw that indicated she had probably had a face lift. Her eyes were as scornful as ever, her hand as cool when she put it briefly into mine.

"Why are we being dragged to this godforsaken place when everything could easily have been sent in the post?"

She did not ask me how I was, tell me where she had come from, mention Aunt Kestrel.

I said I supposed the solicitor was following our aunt's instructions and I heard again the short, hard little laugh I had got to know so well.

She sat down and glanced at me with little interest.

"God I hated that place," she said. "What on earth am I going to do with it? Sell it, that's the only possible thing, though whoever would be mad enough to want it? Do you remember those awful poky little rooms she gave us in the attics?"

"Yes. Do you . . ."

"And that woman . . . Mrs. . . . pinch-face . . ."

"Mullen."

"You were a very meek little boy."

I did not remember myself as that, though I knew I had been intimidated by Leonora, and also quite careful in manner and behavior, anxious not to cause any trouble.

"Quite the goody-goody."

"Whereas you . . ."

The laugh again.

"God I hated it. Nothing to do, the wind howling, boring books, no games."

"Oh but there were games—don't you remember playing endless Bagatelle?"

"No. I remember there was nothing to do at all."

"You had your birthday while we were there."

"Did I? What, eight, nine, something like that?"

"Nine."

"Do you have children?"

"No, I'm afraid . . ."

"Nor do I yet but I'm expecting one, God help me."

I must have looked startled.

"Yes, yes, I know, I'm forty-three, stupid thing to do."

"Your husband . . ."

"Archer? American, of course. He's twenty years

younger, so I suppose he ought to have a family but this will be it, he's lucky to get one."

She told me that he was her third husband, an international hotelier, that they had flats in New York and Paris but spent most of the time traveling.

"I live in grand hotels, out of a suitcase. Where is the man?"

Every so often I caught sight of the child Leonora inside this brittle, well-dressed woman, but she was more or less completely masked by what, oddly, seemed to me a falsely adult air. I wondered if she still had terrors and a temper. I was about to find out.

James Maundeville came back, full of apologies. Leonora made a gesture of annoyance. He picked up a file on his desk, and took out the usual long envelope in which solicitors file Last Will and Testaments.

"I won't read the preamble; it's just the familiar disclaimers. Mrs. Dickinson had savings and investments which formed the capital on whose interest she lived for many years but that capital was considerably eroded by the needs of her last year in a nursing home. The remainder amounts to some twelve thousand pounds. There are no valuables—a few items of personal jewelry worth perhaps a thousand pounds all told. But she expressly asked that you should both, as her sole legatees, come here to learn not so much what she has left but the somewhat—er—eccentric—conditions attached. I did not draw up Mrs. Dickinson's will, my father did and I'm afraid he has been suffering from dementia for the last eighteen months and so I wasn't able to discuss this with him."

He looked up at us both. His face was serious but there was a flicker of amusement there too. He was a good looking, pleasant man with a strong trace of the local accent in his educated voice.

Leonora sat with one stockinged leg crossed tightly over the other. I tried to imagine her as the mother of a child, but simply could not. I felt sorry for any offspring she might produce.

"Mrs. Dickinson left her entire estate, which includes everything I mentioned above—the money, pieces of jewelry and so on, plus Iyot House, with all its contents— with an exception which I will come to—" He cleared his throat nervously, and hesitated a moment before continuing, "to Mr. Edward Cayley . . ." A glance at me.

"The exception . . ."

BUT BEFORE HE could read on, Leonora let out an animal cry of rage and distress. I had heard it once before. The voice was older, the tone a little deeper, but otherwise her furious howl was exactly the same as the one she had uttered the night of her birthday when she had opened the doll Aunt Kestrel had brought for her from London.

Mr. Maundeville looked alarmed. I got up, and took Leonora's arm but she shook me off and raged at us both, her words difficult to make out but not difficult to guess at. He proffered water, but then simply sat waiting for the outburst to run its course.

Leonora was like someone possessed. She raged against Aunt Kestrel, me, the solicitor, raged about unfairness and deceit and hinted at fraud and collusion. The house should have been hers, the estate hers, though we could not discover why she was so sure. Desire, want, getting what she believed ought to be hers—simple greed, these were what drove her, as they had driven her in childhood and, I saw now, throughout her life.

In the end, I persuaded her to calm and quieten by saying that whatever Aunt Kestrel had willed, once the estate was mine I could do what I liked and there was no question of not sharing things with her fairly. This stopped her.

Mr. Maundeville had clearly formed a poor impression of Leonora and wanted her out of his sight. He went back to the Will.

"Mrs. Dickinson has left one item to you, Mrs. Sebastian. I confess I do not fully understand the wording.

"My niece Leonora should have the china doll which was my 9th birthday gift to her and for which she was so ungrateful, in the hope that she will learn to treat it, as she should treat everyone, with more kindness and care."

He sat back and laid down the paper. Leonora's hands were shaking, her face horribly pale and contorted with fury. But she said no word. She got up and walked out, leaving me to smooth things over, explain and apologize as best I could and follow her into the square.

She was nowhere to be seen. I wandered about for some time looking for her but in the end I gave up, and drove back out to Iyot House. Of course, I intended to share my inheritance with Leonora. I could not in conscience have done anything else, though she had made me angry and tempted me to change my mind and keep everything, simply out of frustration at her behavior. She was the child she had been and if no one else could bring her face to face with her unpleasant character, perhaps I could.

But whatever I decided, I was determined that she should have the wretched doll. As I drove across the fen something was hovering just under the surface of my mind, as it had been hovering all the previous night, but when I had heard Maundeville read out the clause about the doll, something had bubbled nearer to the surface, and I had remembered Leonora's outburst that terrible evening, Aunt Kestrel's hurt and annoyance, and then something else, something closer to me, or rather, to my eight-year-old self.

The sun was shining and there was a brisk breeze. As I went toward the gates to the yard, I saw that they had been opened already and that a large car was parked there. Leonora was ahead of me.

The house felt cold and bleak, and smelled more strongly of dust and emptiness than I had remembered from the previous day. I went inside and called out. At first, there was no reply, but as I went up the stairs, calling again, I heard Leonora's voice.

She was in the attics, standing at the window of her old room, looking down.

"How weird," she said. "It's smaller and dingier than I remember and it reeks of unhappiness."

"Not mine," I said, "I was never unhappy here though I was sometimes bored and sometimes lonely. But I thought you and I had quite a happy time that summer."

She shook her head, not so much in disagreement as if she were puzzled.

"Did you understand that nonsense about a doll?" She spoke dismissively.

"Anyhow, why should I care tuppence about it, whatever she meant? The old woman was obviously demented. But now, I suggest the only thing to be done here is for you to sell the house and divide the money between us. God knows, I wouldn't want to come back again and I doubt if you do."

But I had stopped listening to her. We were in my old attic room now and I had seen the cupboard in the wall again. And I remembered I had first hidden the doll there. I stood transfixed, a small boy lying in the bed and hearing the rustle of the tissue paper. I was looking again inside the white cardboard box and seeing the smashed china head and the blue, sightless yet staring eyes, and feeling sorry for the doll even though, like my cousin, I did not care for it very much. I had been frightened too, for what doll could cry, let alone move so that its tissue covering rustled?

꙳

SHE HAD GONE back down the stairs and I could hear her snapping up one of the blinds in Aunt Kestrel's sitting room.

"Come on," I said, "I know where it is."

"What are you babbling about now?"

But I was out and down the path to the gate. I called back to her over my shoulder. "I'm going to get it for you."

I WAS NOT in control of myself. I felt pushed on by the urge to find out if I was right, get the doll and give it back to Leonora, as if I could never rest again until I did. It seemed to be the doll that was urging me, demanding to be rescued and returned to its owner, but I knew now that it, or perhaps, the memory of it, had possessed me for all those years. I felt partly that I wanted to be rid of all trace of it, partly responsible because only I knew where it was and could rescue it. I did not pause to consider how sane this all was, or that I was behaving bizarrely, a man in his forties who had never before been under the influence of something I could only fear was other than human.

Sixteen

"Edward? Where are you? What in God's name are you doing?"

"Here. Over here."

Dusk was rapidly gathering now, the sky still light on the horizon, but the land darkening. I had reached the churchyard and was clambering over the hassocks of thick grass and the prone gravestones, to reach the low stone wall. I could hear Leonora calling after me and then her footsteps coming down the path but I did not wait. I knew what I must do and she was no longer any part of it. I was acting alone and under the urging of something quite other.

I found what I thought was the nearest gravestone and then, to my surprise, the patch of soil that no grass had managed to invade. There were pine needles and a few small fir cones. It was hard and bone dry there and I had nothing with which to dig but my own bare hands. But I knelt down and started to scrabble away at the surface.

Leonora appeared beside me, breathing hard, as if she had been running, but more out of fear than exertion I knew.

"Edward?"

"I have to do this. I have to do it."

"Do what? Dig a hole? Find something down there?"

"Both." I sat back on my heels. "But it's hopeless; I can make no impression at all. I need a spade." And I remembered the feel of the small tin spade in my hands, the blunted, rusty edge with which I had dug into this same ground. I cannot have gone down far.

I got up and went round the side of the church, finding what I needed almost at once—the shed in which whoever maintained the churchyard and dug the occasional grave kept his things. The padlock was undone. I found what I needed easily enough, wondering how much it was used; Iyot Lock was a hamlet of so few houses—there cannot have been many burials.

LEONORA HAD FOLLOWED me, obviously not wanting to be alone, and now was beside the wall, looking down. I pushed the blade into the earth with all my strength but it was extremely hard ground and yielded little. I scraped away as best I could, and after a short time the soil loosened. There were some tree roots which must have spread in the many years since I was last here and which made my task harder but I did not have to go very deep before I bumped against something caught beneath one of them. It was not hard, but felt compressed.

I threw down the spade and knelt on the grass. Leonora was standing nearby, and as I glanced up I saw that she was looking with alarm at me, as if she feared I had gone mad.

"It's all right," I said, in a falsely cheerful voice, "I told you I would find it for you."

"Find what? What on earth are you doing, Edward, and should you be digging about in a churchyard? Isn't that wickedness or illegal or some such thing? You could be digging up someone's grave."

"I am," I said.

It seems insane indeed, now I look back, but at the time I was possessed by the need to find out if I was right, and get Leonora what my aunt had willed her. She was right, as she had screeched in the solicitor's office, she had been cut out of the rest of the inheritance and only left the wretched doll in what was perhaps the one mean-spirited gesture our aunt had ever made. Her childhood behavior over the birthday doll, her spoiled tantrum and violent rejection of it, when Kestrel had gone to buy it especially, to make up for disappointment, must have rankled for years—unless she had written her will shortly after it had all happened. Either way, she intended Leonora to be taught a lesson but I was not going to indulge in that sort of tit-for-tat gesture. I would tell Leonora that I planned to give her exactly half the money we eventually achieved.

This had all become some sort of game that had gone too far. I knew that well enough as I knelt on the ground and felt around with both my hands in the space under the tree root. I soon came upon a damp lump of something and gradually used my fingers to ease it away from the soil.

The white cardboard box had rotted away over the years and then adhered like clay to the contents, and as I took it in my hands, I could feel the shape beneath. It was a slimy grey mess.

It was also almost completely dark and I laid the object on the ground while I hastily covered the soil back over the shallow place I had cleared.

"Come on, back to the house. I can't see anything here."

"Edward, what have you done?"

"I told you—I have retrieved your inheritance."

I carried it carefully down the dark road back to Iyot House. It felt unpleasant, slimy and with clots of soil adhering to the wet mush of cardboard.

I do not know that I had thought particularly about the state the doll would be in after being buried for so long. Certainly the way the box had disintegrated was no surprise—the very fact that it was there at all was remarkable. If you had asked me I suppose I would have said the doll would be very dirty, perhaps unrecognizable as a doll, but undamaged—china or pot or plastic, whatever it was actually made of, would not have rotted like the box.

꙰

I WENT INTO the old kitchen, found a dust sheet and laid it on the deal table. Leonora seemed to be as intrigued as I was, though also distinctly alarmed.

"How did you know where to look? What on earth was it doing buried there in the churchyard?"

I half remembered that something had happened to startle me and make me want the wretched thing out of the house but the details were hazy now.

"I think I had a dream about it."

"Don't be ridiculous."

But now we were both looking at the filthy soil-coated object on the table. I found a bowl of cold water, an ancient cloth and a blunt kitchen knife and began to rinse and scrape away carefully.

"I don't know why you are doing this. Is it full of money?"

"I doubt it."

"No, of course it isn't. I don't want it, can't you understand Edward? This is a stupid game. For God's sake, throw it in a bin and let's get out of this awful house."

All the same, she could not help watching me intently as I worked patiently away. It did not take me long to get rid of the wet sodden mush of soil and cardboard and then my fingers touched the hard object beneath. I emptied and re-filled the bowl of water and rinsed and re-rinsed. First the body of the china doll appeared, dirty but apparently intact.

"I know Aunt Kestrel would have wanted you to have it in as near perfect condition as we can get it, Leonora!"

She was transfixed by the sight. "I remember it," she said after a moment. "It's coming back to me—that awful night. I remember expecting it to be something so special, so beautiful, and this hideous china baby came out of the box."

"Do you remember what kind of a doll you had wanted? I drew a picture of it for you."

She told me, though some of the detail was inaccurate, but the bridal princess came to life as she spoke.

I was anxious not to damage this doll, so I worked even more slowly as I got most of the outer dirt away and then I carried it to the tap and rinsed it under a trickle of water. If I had stopped to think how ridiculous I must have looked—how oddly we were both behaving indeed, perhaps I would not have gone on. I wish now that indeed I had not, that I had left the doll covered and buried under the earth in its sorry grave. But it was too late for that.

"There," I said at last. "Let us see your treasure, Leonora!" I spoke in a light and jocular tone, the last time I was to do so that night and for many others.

I carried the doll, still wet but clean, to the table and laid it down directly under the light. I had pushed all the rubbish into a bin so there was now just the scrubbed, pale wooden table top and the doll lying on it.

We both looked. And then Leonora's hand flew to her mouth as she made a dreadful low sound, not a cry, not a wail, hardly a human sound but something almost animal.

I looked into the face of the doll and then I too saw what she had seen.

WHEN WE HAD both looked at it last we were children and the doll was a baby doll, with staring bright blue eyes, a painted rosebud mouth and a smooth china face, neck, arms, legs and body. It was an artificial-looking thing but it was as like a human baby as any doll can ever be.

Now, we both stared in horror at the thing on the table in front of us. It was not a baby, but a wizened old woman, a crone, with a few wisps of twisted greasy grey hair, a mouth slightly open to reveal a single black tooth, and the face gnarled and wrinkled like a tree trunk, with lines and pockmarks. It was sallow, the eyes were sunken and the lids creased with age, the lips thin and hard.

I let out a small cry, and then said, "But of course. This isn't your doll. Someone has changed it for this hideous thing."

"How?" Leonora asked in a whisper, "When? Why? Whoever knew it had been buried there?"

I would have tried to come up with a thousand explanations but I could not even begin. For as I looked at the dreadful, aged doll, I realized that the crack in the skull and the hollow beneath it, which had come when Leonora had hurled it at the wall, were exactly the same, still jagged like a broken egg, though dirty round the edges from being in the earth.

This was not a replacement doll, put there by someone—though God knows who—with a sick sense of humor. This was the first doll, the bland-faced baby. The crack in its skull was exactly as it had been, I was sure of that. The body was the same size and shape though oddly crooked and with chicken-claw hands and feet and a yellow, loose-skinned neck. This was the doll Aunt Kestrel had given Leonora. It was the same doll.

But the doll had grown old.

I MANAGED TO FIND some brandy in Aunt Kestrel's old sitting-room cupboard, and poured us both a generous glassful. After that, I locked up the house, leaving everything as it was, and drove Leonora back to Cold Eeyle and the hotel, for she was in no state to do anything for herself. She sat beside me shaking and occasionally letting out a little cry, after which her body would give a long convulsive shudder. I insisted that a doctor be called out, as she was in the early stages of pregnancy, and stayed until he had left, saying that she needed sleep and peace but that she and the child were essentially unharmed.

I spent a terrible night, full of nightmares in which dolls, old ones and young ones mixed together, came at me out of thick fog, alternately laughing and crying. I woke at six and went straight out, driving fast to Iyot House through a drear, cold morning.

The doll which had grown old was where we had left it, on the kitchen table, and still old and wizened, like a witch from a fairy tale. I had half expected to find that it had all been some dreadful illusion and that the doll was still a baby, just filthy and distorted by having been buried in the damp earth for so long.

But the earth had done nothing to the doll, other than ruining its cardboard coffin. The doll was a crone, looking a hundred years old or a thousand, ancient and repulsive.

I did as I had done before, went alone to the churchyard and buried it, this time wrapped in an old piece of sheeting. I dug as deep as I could and replaced the earth firmly on top. When I had finished I felt a sense of release. Whatever had happened, the wretched, hideous thing would never emerge again and there was an end.

彡

BUT SHE HAD power to haunt me. I dreamed of the aged doll for many nights, many months. I worried over what had happened and how. Sometimes, I half convinced myself that we had both imagined it, Leonora and I, for, of course, an inanimate object, a doll made of pot, could not age. The dirt and soil, added to years in the damp ground, had changed the features—that was quite understandable.

In the end, the image faded from my mind and reason took over.

彡

LEONORA DISAPPEARED FROM my life once more, though I heard in a roundabout way that she had returned to the Far East and her hotelier husband.

As for me, I was about to pack up Iyot House and put it up for sale, when I was asked to go abroad myself, to do a special job for a foreign government and it was such a major and exciting challenge that the house in the fens and everything to do with it went from my mind.

PART FOUR

Seventeen

I was to spend three or four months in the city of Szargesti, a once-handsome place in the old Eastern Europe. It had an old and beautiful center, but much of that had been demolished during the 1970s, to make way for wide roads on which only presidential and official cars could travel, vast, ugly new civic buildings and a monstrous presidential palace. The Old Town was medieval, and had once housed a jewelry quarter, book-binders and small printers, leather workers, and various tradesmen who kept the ancient buildings upright. Many had been wood and lathe, with astonishing painted panels on their façades. There had been a cathedral and other old churches, as well as a synagogue, for a large section of the original population of Szargesti had been Jewish. The place had been vandalized and the demolition had proceeded in a brutal and haphazard fashion, alongside the hurried erection of a new civic center. But the Prague Spring had come to Szargesti, the president had been exiled, many of his cronies executed, and both demolition and building had come to an abrupt halt. Huge craters stood in the middle of streets, blocks of flats were left half in ruins, the machinery which had been pulling them down left rusting in their midst. It was a testament to grand designs and the lust for power of ignorant men. I am an adviser on the conservation of ancient buildings and sometimes, on whole areas, as in the case of Szargesti. My task was to identify and catalog what was left, photograph it and make certain that nothing else was destroyed, and then to give the city advice on how to shore up, preserve, rebuild with care.

꙳

I KNEW THAT the Old Town, with its medieval buildings—houses, shops, workshops—was the most important area and in urgent need of conservation and repair. I had quickly come to love the place, with its small, intimate squares, narrow cobbled alleyways, beautiful, often ramshackle four-story buildings with their neglected but still beautiful frescoes and wall paintings. The best way of getting to know a place is simply to wander and this is almost all I did for the first couple of weeks, taking dozens of photographs. Every evening I returned to my hotel to make copious notes, but after I had come to know the city a little better I would often stay out late, find a café in the back streets, drink a beer or a coffee and watch what little street life there was. People were still uncertain, ground down by years of a brutal dictatorship and most of them kept safely inside their homes after dark. But one warm summer evening I went into the Old Town and a square I had chanced upon earlier in the day, and which had some of the most beautiful and undamaged houses I had so far discovered. It would once have housed traders and craftsmen in precious metals whose workshops were situated beneath their houses. On the corner I passed an old stone water trough with an elaborately carved iron tap stood beside it. Horses would have drunk here, but the water had probably also been carried away in buckets, for use in smelting.

Now, the heavy wooden doors and iron shutters of the workshops were closed and some were padlocked, and those padlocks were rusty and broken. Many of the upper rooms had gaping dark spaces where windows had fallen out.

THERE WAS A small café with a few tables on the cobbles. The barman appeared the moment I sat down, brought my drink and a small dish of smoked sausage, but then returned to the doorway and watched me until I began to feel uneasy. I had no need to be, I knew, and I tried to enjoy the quietness, the last of the sunshine and the way the shadows lengthened, slipping across the cobbles toward me. The old women who had been sitting on a bench chatting left. The tobacconist came out with a long pole and rattled down his shutters. The beer was good. The sausage tasted of woodsmoke.

I continued to feel uneasy and strangely restless, alone

in the darkening square. So far as I knew, only the waiter was looking at me but I had the odd sense that there were others, watching from the blanked-out windows and hidden corners. I have always believed that places with a long history, especially those in which terrible events have taken place, retain something of those times, some trace in the air, just as I have been in many a cathedral all over the world and sensed the impress of centuries of prayers and devotions. Places are often filled with their own pasts and exude a sense of them, an atmosphere of great good or great evil, which can be picked up by anyone sensitive to their surroundings. Even a dog's hackles can rise in places reputed to be haunted. I am not an especially credulous man but I believe in these things because I have experienced them. I am not afraid of the dark and it was not the evening shadows that were making me nervous now. Certainly I had no fear of potential attackers or of spies leftover from the city's past. Thank God those days were over and Szargesti was struggling to come to terms with the new freedoms.

I finished my beer and got up.

The air was still warm and the stars were beginning to brighten in the silky sky as I walked slowly round the square, where the cobbles gave way to stone paving. Every window was dark and shuttered. The only sound was that of my own footsteps.

Here and there an old stable door stood ajar, revealing cobbles on which straw was still scattered though the horses had long gone. I passed a music shop, a cobbler's, and one tiny frontage displaying pens and parchment. All were locked up, and dark. Then, in the middle of the narrowest, dimmest alley, where the walls of the houses bulged across almost to meet one another, I saw a yellowish light coming from one of the windows and nearing it, I found a curious shop.

The window was dusty, making it difficult to see much of what was inside but I could make out shelves and an ancient counter. No attempt had been made to display goods attractively—the window held a jumble of objects piled together. I put my hand on the latch and at once heard the ring of an old-fashioned bell.

A VERY SMALL old man was behind the mahogany counter, his skin paper pale and almost transparent over the bones of his cheeks and skull. He had tufts of yellow-white hair, yellow-white eyebrows and a jeweler's glass screwed into one eye, with which he was examining a round silver box, dulled and stained with verdigris.

He raised a finger in recognition of my entrance, but continued to peer down at the object, and so I looked round me at the stock, which was crammed onto the shelves, spilled out of drawers, displayed in glass cabinets. The floor was of uncovered oak boards, polished and worn by the passage of feet over years.

The lower shelves contained small leather bound books, boxes of various sizes with metal hasps, dulled by the same verdigris as the box being scrutinized, wooden trays with what looked like puzzles fitted into them, a couple of musical boxes. Higher up, I saw wooden cabinets with sets of narrow drawers, each labeled in the old Cyrillic alphabet which had not been used in the country for almost a century. A dolls' house stood on the floor beside me, its eaves and roof modeled on those of the buildings in the square, its front hanging half-off its single hinge. Beside it was a child-sized leather trunk, the leather rubbed and lifting here and there. I glanced at the old man but now he had set the box on a scrap of dark blue velvet set down on the counter and was peering at it even more intently through his eyeglass, I thought perhaps trying to make out some pattern or inscription.

I turned back to the dolls' house and trunk and as I did so, I heard a sound which at first I took to be the scratching of a mouse in the skirting somewhere—I hoped a mouse, and not a rat. It stopped and then, as I put out my hand to touch the front of the wooden house, started again, and though it was still very soft, I knew that it was not the noise made by any sort of rodent. I could not tell exactly where it originated—it seemed to be coming from the darkness somewhere, behind me, or to one side—I could not quite pin down the direction. It was a rustling of some kind—perhaps the sound made when the wind blows through branches or reeds, perhaps the movement of long grass. Yet it was not altogether like those sounds. It stopped again. I looked at the old man but he was crouching over his box, his narrow back half bent, shoulders hunched.

I waited. It came again. A soft, insistent, rustling sound. Like paper. Someone was rustling paper—perhaps sheets of tissue paper. I turned my head to one corner, then the other but the sound did not quite come from there, or there, or from anywhere.

Perhaps it was inside my own head.

The old man sat up abruptly, put down the eyeglass and looked directly at me. His eyes were the watery grey of the sea on a dull day, dilute and pale.

"Good evening," he said in English. "Is it something special you look for, because in a moment, I close."

"Thank you, no. I was just interested to find a shop here and open at this time."

"Ah."

"You sell many different things. What do you call yourself?"

"A restorer."

"But so am I!"

"Toys?"

"No, ancient buildings. Like those in this quarter. I'm an architectural conservator."

He nodded.

"Little is beyond repair but my job is more easy than yours."

He gestured round. I had begun to notice that many of the objects on his shelves and even standing around the floor were old toys, mostly of wood, some painted elaborately, some simply carved. As well as the dolls' house I had already seen, there were others, and then a fort, many soldiers in the original military uniforms of the country's past, a wooden truck, a railway engine and many boxes of different sizes and shapes. A lot of them had clearly been gathering dust for years. I looked down at the cloth on which the miniature silver box was standing.

"This has been chased by hand, the most expert hand." He offered the eyeglass for me to examine it. "The work of a fine craftsman. It was found on the dresser of a dolls' house—but I think it was not a toy item. Please, look."

I did so. There was some intricate patterning forming the border and in the center, a night sky with moon and stars and clouds, with a swirl of movement suggesting a wild wind.

"Certainly not a toy." I handed back the eyeglass. "Marvelous workmanship."

"This old part of Szargesti, were craftsmen who worked in silver many years past, special craftsmen who passed down their skill to younger ones. Now . . ." He sighed. "Almost none left. Skills in danger of death. I do not have these skills. I am only repairer of toys. Please, look round. You have some children?"

I shook my head. I assumed that everything here was waiting for repair and not for sale but even old toys, like many other domestic artifacts, tell a conservator something about the times in which they were made and even of the buildings in which they belonged and I poked about a little more, finding treasures behind treasures. But I wondered how long some of them had been lying here and how much longer they would have to wait for the mender's attention. And then I wondered if some of the children who had owned and played with them were now grown-up or even dead, the toys were so old-fashioned.

The old man let me look around, poke into corners, touch and even pick things up without taking any notice of me and I was at the very back of the shop, where it was even darker and dustier, when I heard it again. The faint rustling sound seemed to be coming from something close to me but when I turned, became softer as if it were moving away. I stood very still. The shop was quiet. I heard the rustling again, as if tissue paper were being scrumpled up or unfolded, and now I thought I could trace the sound to somewhere on the floor and quite close to my feet. I bent down but it was very dark and I saw nothing unusual, and there was no quick movement of a rodent scuttling away. It stopped. Started again, more softly. Stopped. I took a step or two forward and my foot bumped up against something. I bent down. A cardboard box, about the size to contain a pair of boots, was just in front of me, the lid apparently tied on with stout string. It was as I put my hand out to touch it that I felt an iciness down my spine, and a sudden moment of fear. I was sure that I was remembering something but I had no idea what. Deep in my subconscious mind a cardboard box like this one had a place but in what way or from what stage of my life I did not know.

I stood up hastily and as I did so, the rustling began again. It was coming from inside the box.

But I did not have a chance to try to trace the source of the sound, even if I was sure that I wanted to do so, because the old man unnerved me by saying:

"You are looking for a doll I think."

I opened my mouth to say that I was not, had just

been drawn into the shop out of curiosity, but I realized that was not true.

"Look there."

I looked. In a cabinet just above my head was the doll, the exact, the same doll, which Leonora had yearned for all those years ago, the doll she had described in such detail and which I had tried to draw for her as some sort of compensation.

The Indian Princess, in her rich garments, shining jewels, sequins, beads, embroidery, sparkling with gold and silver, ruby and emerald, pearl and diamond, was sitting on some sort of velvet chair with a high, crested back, her face bland and serene, her veil sprinkled with silver and gold suns, moons and stars. She was not a doll for a child, not a doll to be played with, dressed and undressed, fed and pushed about in an old pram, she was far too fine, too regal, too formal. But I knew that this was the doll my cousin had yearned for so desperately and that I had no choice but to buy it—it had been placed here for just that reason. Even as the thought flashed across my mind, I was almost embarrassed, it was so ridiculous, and yet some part of me believed that it was true.

The old man was still tapping away calmly, smiling a little.

"Are your dolls for sale?"

"You wish to buy that one." It was not a question.

He glanced at me, the very centers of his eyes steel-bright, fixed and all-seeing.

Now, he had come round the counter and was unlocking the cabinet. A shiver rippled down my back as he reached inside and took hold of the Indian Princess. He did not ask me if this was the one I wanted, simply took it down, locked the cabinet again and then laid the doll on the counter.

"I have the exact box." He retreated into the shadows where I could just make out a door that stood ajar. My back was icy cold now. The shop was very quiet and somewhere in that quietness, I heard the rustling sound again.

He came back with the doll, boxed, lidded, tied with string and handed it over to me. I paid him and fled, out into the alley under the tallow light of the gas lamp, the coffin-like box under my arm. Through the window, I could make out the old man, behind the counter. He did not look up.

When I got back to the hotel, I pushed the doll under the bed in my room and went down to the cheerful bar, with its red shaded lamps and buzz of talk, and had a couple of brandies to try to rid myself of the unpleasant chill through my body, and a general sense of malaise. Gradually, I calmed. I began to try to work out why I had heard the rustling sound and what it had meant, but soon gave up. It could not have had anything to do with any of the similar sounds I had heard before. I was in another country, a different place.

I went to bed, fortified by the brandy, and was on the very cusp of sleep when I sat straight up, my heart thumping in my chest. The rustling sound had started up again and as I listened in horror, I realized that it was coming from close to hand. I lay down again and then it was louder. I sat up, and it faded.

Either the rustling was in my own head—or rather, in my ears, some sort of tinnitus—or it was coming from underneath the bed.

＊

THAT NIGHT MY dreams were full of cascading images of dolls, broken, damaged, buried, covered in dirt, labeled, lying on shelves, being hammered and glued and tapped. In the middle of it all, the memory of Leonora's twisted and angry face as she hurled the unwanted doll at the fireplace, and floating somewhere behind, the old man with the gimlet eyes.

I woke in a sweat around dawn and pulled the box from under the bed where I had left it, the string still carefully knotted. I did not want it in my sight, but I was sure that if I disposed of the doll I would have cause to regret it and first thing the next morning I took it to the post office. I had addressed it to myself in London but changed my mind at the last moment, and sent it instead to Iyot House. The reasons were mainly practical yet I was also sending the doll there because it seemed right and where it naturally belonged.

I felt relief when it was out of my hands. I had kept it and yet I had not.

Eighteen

Some months passed, during which I heard via an announcement in *The Times* that Leonora had given birth to a daughter. I returned to England, but for the next year or so I was constantly traveling between London and Szargesti, absorbed in my work and I gave thought to little else.

And then I received a letter from the solicitor, telling me that Leonora wished to be in touch with me urgently. She had written via Iyot House but received no reply. Might he forward my address to her?

By the time I did receive a letter, I was married, I had finished my work in Szargesti, and embarked on a new project connected with English cathedrals. Leonora was far from my mind.

Dear Edward

I write to you from the depths of despair. I am unsure how much you know of what has happened to me since we last met. Briefly, I have a daughter, who is now two years old, and named Frederica, after her father and my beloved husband, Frederic, who died very suddenly. We were in Switzerland. In short, he has left me penniless; the hotels are on the verge of bankruptcy thanks to bad advice. I did not know a thing. How could I have known when Frederic protected me from everything? And now my daughter has a grave illness.

I have nowhere to go, nowhere to live. I am staying with friends out of their kindness and pity but that must come to an end.

In short, I am throwing myself on your generosity and asking if you would allow me to have Iyot House in which to live, though God knows I hate the place and would not want to set foot inside it again, if this were not my only possible home. Perhaps we could make it habitable.

If you have already disposed of it then I ask if you could share some of the proceeds with me so that I can buy a place in which my sick child and I can live.

Please reply c/o the poste restante address and tell me urgently what you can do. We are cousins, after all,

Affectionately
Leonora.

I had done nothing about Iyot House and after I told my wife the gist of the story she agreed at once that, of course, Leonora and her daughter should live there for as long as they wished.

"It's been locked up for years. I don't know what

state it will be in and it was never the most—welcoming of houses anyway."

"But surely you can get people to go in and make sure it is clean and that there hasn't been any damage . . . that the place isn't flooded? Then she can make the best of it . . . Anything other than being homeless."

I agreed but wondered as I did so if Leonora had told me the full truth, if she had indeed been left literally penniless and without the means to put a roof over her head. Her letter was melodramatic and slightly hysterical, entirely in character. Catherine chided me with heartlessness when I tried to explain and perhaps she was right. But then, she did not know Leonora.

Nevertheless, I wrote and said that she could have the house, that I would put anything to rights before she arrived, and would come to see her when I could manage it.

༄

I HAD TO travel to Cambridge a few days later, and I arranged to make a detour via Iyot House. It was September, the weather golden, the corn ripe in the fields, the vast skies blue with mare's tail clouds streaked high. At this time of year the area is so open, so fresh-faced, with nothing hidden for miles, everything was spread out before me as I drove. It is still an isolated place. No one has developed new housing clusters and the villages and hamlets remain quite self-contained, not spreading, not even seeming to relate to one another. Apart from some drainage, square miles had not changed since I was an eight-year-old boy being driven from the railway station on my first visit to Iyot House. I remembered how I had felt—interested and alert to my surroundings, and yet also lonely and apprehensive, determined but fearful. And when I had first glimpsed the place, I had shivered, though I had not known why. It was as though nothing was exactly as it seemed to be, like a place in a story, there were other dimensions, shadows, secrets, the walls seemed to be very slightly crooked. I was not an especially imaginative child, so I was even more aware of what I felt.

The house smelled of dust and emptiness but not, to my surprise, of damp or mold, and although everything seemed a little more faded and neglected, there was no interior damage. I pulled up some of the blinds and opened a couple of windows. A bird had fallen down one of the chimneys and its body lay in the empty fireplace, grass sprouted on window ledges. But the place was just habitable, if I found someone to clean and reorder it. Leonora would at least have a roof over her head for however long she and the child needed it.

I had noticed that the box I had sent from Szargesti was in the porch, tucked safely out of the weather. I took it inside and decided that I would place it upstairs in the small room off the main bedroom which Leonora might well choose for her daughter. The attics were too far away and lonely for a small child.

I put the box on the shelf, hesitating about whether to take the doll out and display it, or leave it as a surprise. In the end I removed all the outer wrapping and string, but left the box closed, so that the little girl could have the fun of opening it.

Nineteen

I have written this account in a reasonably calm, even detached frame of mind. I have remembered that first strange childhood visit to Iyot House in some detail without anxiety and although it distressed me a little to recall the unpleasantness over the doll with the aged face, its burial and exhumation, and Leonora's violent tempers, I have written with a steady hand. Events were peculiar, strange things happened, and yet I have looked back steadily and without falling prey to superstitions and night terrors. I have always believed that the odd happenings could be put down to coincidence or perhaps the effects of mood and atmosphere. I suppose I believed myself to be a rational man.

But reason does not help me now that I come to the climax of the story, and as I remember and as I write, I feel as if there is no ground beneath my feet, that I might disintegrate at any moment, that my flesh will dissolve. I feel afraid but I do not know of what. I feel helpless and at the mercy of strange events and forces which not only can I not explain away but in which I do not believe.

Yet what happened, happened, all of it, and the end lies in the beginning, in our childhood. But the blame is not mine, the blame is all Leonora's.

WORK PREOCCUPIED ME and then Catherine and I took a trip to New York, so that I was not in touch with Leonora until she had been living in Iyot House for some weeks.

It was one day in December when I had finished some more work in Cambridge earlier than I had expected, and I decided to drive across to Iyot House and either beg a bed for the night there or carry on to the inn at Cold Eeyle. I tried to telephone my cousin in advance but there was no reply and so I simply set off. It was early dusk and the sun was flame and ruby red in the clearest of skies as I went toward the fens. Once off the trunk roads, it was as quiet as ever. There were few lock keeper's cottages occupied now—that had been the one major change since my boyhood—but here and there a light glowed through windows, and the glint of these or of the low sun touched the black deep slow-running waters in river and dike. The church at Iyot Lock stood out as a beacon in the flat landscape for miles ahead, the last of the sun touching its gilded flying angels on all four corners of the tower.

It was beautiful and seemed so serene an aspect that

I was moved and felt happier to be coming here than ever before. So much of what we imagine is a product of an ill mood, a restless night, indigestion, or the vagaries of the weather and I began to feel certain that all the previous events at Iyot House had been caused by one or other of these, or by other equally fleeting outside circumstances. Empty houses breed fantasies, bleak landscapes lend themselves to fearful imaginings. Only lie awake on a windy night and hear a branch tap-tap-tapping on a casement to understand at once what I mean.

I DREW UP outside the house—the gate to the back entrance was locked and barred, so I parked in the road and got out. There was a light on in the sitting room, behind drawn curtains, one upstairs and possibly one at the very back. I did not want to startle Leonora, for she would presumably not expect callers on an early December evening, so I banged the door of the car shut a couple of times, and made some noise opening the gate and tramping up the path to the front door. I pulled the bell out hard and heard it jangle through the house.

Those few moments I stood waiting outside in the cold darkness were, I now realize, the last truly calm and untroubled ones I was ever to spend. Never again did I feel so steady and equable, never again did I anticipate nothing ahead of me of a frightening, unnerving and inexplicable kind. After this, I would be anxious and apprehensive no matter where I was or what I did. That something terrible, though I never knew what, was about to happen, in the next few moments, or hours, or days, I was always certain. I did not sleep well again, and if I feared for my own health and sanity, how much more did I fear for those of my family.

The front door opened. Leonora was standing there and in the poor light of the hall she looked far older, less smart, less assured, than she had ever been. When she held the door open for me in silence, and I stepped inside, I could see her better and my first impression was strengthened. The old Leonora had been well-dressed and groomed, elegant, sophisticated, hard, someone whose expression veered between fury and defiance, with an occasional prolonged sulkiness.

Tonight, she looked ten years older, was without make-up and her hair rolled into a loose bun at the back of her neck was thickly banded with grey. She seemed exhausted, her eyes oddly without expression, and her dress was plain, black, unbecoming.

"I hope I haven't startled you. I don't imagine you get many night callers. I did try to call you."

"The phone is out of service. You'd better come into the kitchen. I can make tea. Or there might be a drink in the house somewhere."

I followed her across the hall. Nothing seemed to have changed. The old furniture, pictures, curtains, carpet were still in place, as if they were everlasting and could never be worn out.

"Frederica is in here. It's the warmest room. I can't afford to heat the whole house."

We went down the short passageway to the kitchen. It was dimly lit. Electricity was expensive.

"Frederica, stand up please. Here is a visitor."

The child was seated at the kitchen table with her back to me. I saw that she looked tall for her age but extremely thin and that she had no hair and inevitably, the word "cancer" came to me. She had had some terrible version of it and the treatment had made her bald and I felt sorry beyond expression, for her and for my cousin.

And then she got down from her chair, and turned to face me.

For a moment, I felt drained of all energy and consciousness, and almost reached out and grabbed the table to steady myself. But I knew that Leonora's eyes were on me, watching, watching, for just such a reaction, and so I managed to stay upright and clear-headed.

Frederica was about three years old but the face she presented to me now was the face of a wizened old woman. She had a long neck, and her mouth was misshapen, sucked inward like that of an old person without teeth. Her eyes protruded slightly, and she had almost no lashes. Her hands were wrinkled and gnarled at the joints, as if she were ninety years old.

"There is no treatment and no cure."

Leonora's voice was as matter-of-fact as if she had been giving me the name of a plant.

I did not want to stare at the child, but I shuddered to look at her. There was something alien about her. I have never had any reaction to a human being with a disfigurement or disease other than extreme sympathy

and it has always seemed best to try to ignore the out-
ward signs as quickly as possible and address the human
being within. But this was so very different. I felt the
usual recoil, shock, pity but far, far more strongly, I felt
fear, fear and horror. Because this small child had aged
in the way the china doll had aged. And insane and irra-
tional as it seemed, I had no doubt she had aged because
of it. The consequences of Leonora's violent temper and
cruel, spiteful, destructive action all those years ago had
come home to her now.

✄

I DID NOT want to stay at Iyot House. I had a drink
and read a picture book to the little girl, saddened when
Leonora told me in bitterness that she would not live
beyond the age of ten or so. She was a happy, friendly
child with the happy chatter of a three year old coming
so oddly out of that wizened little body.

As I was leaving, Leonora asked me to wait in the
porch. The child had been left playing with a jigsaw
in the kitchen, where I gathered they spent much of
their time, because the rest of the house was so cold
and unwelcoming, though I thought that she might have
made it more cheerful if she had tried.

She came downstairs and handed me the cardboard
box which I had left.

"Take it," she said, "hideous thing. What possessed
you to leave such a thing here?"

"I—It seemed the right place for it, now there is a
child here. Could Frederica not play with it?"

Leonora's face was pinched with a mixture of anger and scorn.

"Get rid of it, for God's sake. Haven't you done enough harm?"

"I? What harm have I done? You were the one who hurled the doll against the fireplace and smashed its head open, you were the one who caused . . ."

I stopped. Whatever crazy imaginings I had ever had, I could not conceivably blame my cousin for bringing such a dreadful fate upon her own child. I had no idea how the face of the broken doll had apparently aged but it was inanimate. It could not extract revenge.

I took the box which Leonora was pushing at me, and went. The front door was slammed and bolted before I had reached the gate.

꙳

THE INN AT Cold Eeyle was as comfortable and snug as ever. I was given my old room, and after a stiff whisky, I dined and then slept well and left a happier man to drive back home the next morning.

Twenty

How to tell the rest of my story? How to explain any of it? I prided myself on being a rational man, on having explained things clearly to myself and come to some understanding of the phenomenon of coincidence. I even studied it a little, via the books of those whose life's work it is, and discovered just how much that was once thought mystical, magical, mysterious, is perfectly easily explained by coincidence, whose arm stretches far further than most people would guess.

Is that how I explain away the hideous events of the next few years? Am I convinced by putting it all down to likely chance?

Of course I am not. Things had happened to me in the past which I had pushed out of mind, buried deep so that I did not need to remember them. I had known then that they were not easily explained away and that the emotions and fears, the forebodings and anxieties that overwhelmed me from time to time were fully justified. Strange and inexplicable things had happened, and hidden forces had shaped events for reasons I did not understand. I also remained certain that Leonora was the lightning conductor for all of them.

~

A LITTLE OVER a year after my last visit to Iyot House my wife Catherine gave birth to a daughter, whom we christened Viola Kestrel. When she was almost three my work took me to India, which I loved, but about which Catherine had mixed feelings. She found the heat and humidity intolerable and the extreme poverty distressed her. But she loved the inhabitants at once, and found much to do helping women and their children in a remote village, where there were no medical facilities and where clothes and people were washed in the great river that flowed through the area. Viola was adored by everyone, and was an easy, smiling child, content to be petted and fussed by a dozen people in succession.

And then she was struck down within a few hours by one of the terrible diseases that ravage this beautiful country. Poor sanitation, contaminated water, easy spread of infection, any or all of them were to blame and in spite of Catherine's care and strict precautions it was perhaps a miracle that the child had not suffered from anything serious earlier.

Viola was very ill indeed, with a high fever, pains in her limbs and an intolerance of light. She was delirious and in great distress and we were in an agony of fear that we would lose her. On the fourth day, she woke with a rash of pox-like spots, raised, and red, all over her face and body. The spots were inflamed and became infected and scabbed, so that her fresh skin and beautiful features were hidden. After a week, handfuls of her beautiful corn-colored hair began to fall out and did not regrow. She was a distressing sight and I think I was the one who felt the loss of her beauty the most. Catherine was absorbed in trying to nurse her, help her struggle through the fevers and relieve her symptoms, and so far as she was concerned that Viola should live, no matter what her eventual condition, was all she asked.

She did live. Slowly the fevers subsided and then ceased, her pain and discomfort eased, and she lay, limp and exhausted but out of danger, on a bed as cool as could be made for her, in a darkened corner. Her rash was less red and raised, but the hideous spots crusted and when they fell off left ugly pockmarks which were deep and unlikely ever to disappear. Her beautiful eyes were dimmed and lost their wonderful color and translucence and seemed to have receded deep into their sockets.

Weeks and then three months went by before she began to regain energy and a little weight, to laugh sometimes and clap her hands when the Indian women who had agonized over her clapped theirs.

WE RETURNED HOME exhausted and chastened, wondering what the future held for our once-perfect daughter, still perfect to us, still overwhelmingly loved, but nevertheless, sadly disfigured. In London we consulted a specialist in tropical diseases, who in turn passed us to a dermatologist, and thence to a plastic surgeon. None of them held out any hope that Viola's scars would ever fade very much. It might be possible for her to have a skin graft when she was older but success was by no means certain and there were risks.

Weeks went by while all this was attended to and we settled back with some difficulty into our old life in England.

It was then that I started to search for some particular files and in hunting, found both these and a white cardboard box. At first I did not recognize it and assumed it belonged to Catherine. I set it down on my work table, beside some drawings, but then forgot it until the following day, when I walked into my office early in the morning and as I saw it, remembered immediately where it had come from and what it held.

I saw Leonora again, in the semi-darkness outside Iyot House, thrusting the box into my hands and telling me, almost screaming at me to take it away. Well, my Viola might enjoy the Indian Princess doll, would recognize it as one of her friends and playmates from the country she still remembered vividly. I untied the loosely knotted string and lifted the lid. The rustle of the tissue paper brought goose flesh up on the back of my neck. It was not a sound I would ever again find pleasant and I pushed it aside quickly, not even liking the feel of it against my fingers.

The Indian Princess doll lay as I remembered her in the

bottom of the coffin-like cardboard box. Her elaborate, richly embroidered and bejeweled clothes, her rings, earrings, bracelets and bangles and beads, her satin and lace and gold and silver braid and trim, were all as I had remembered them. There were just two things that were so very different.

Her thick long black hair had come away here and there, leaving ugly bald patches, and the fallen hair was lying in tufts at the bottom of the box.

And her face and hands, which were all that showed of her skin, were covered in deep and hideous pock-marks and scars. She was no longer a beauty, she was no longer about to be a bride, she was a pariah, a sufferer from a disfiguring disease which would mark her for life, someone from whom everyone turned away, their eyes downcast.